THE TAMING

THE TAMING

ERIC WALTERS

TERESA TOTEN

DOUBLEDAY CANADA

Doubleday Canada and colophon are registered trademarks

Library and Archives of Canada Cataloguing in Publication
Toten, Teresa, 1955-
The taming / Teresa Toten and Eric Walters.
Issued also in electronic format.
ISBN 978-0-385-67658-8
I. Walters, Eric, 1957- II. Title.
PS8589.O6759T35 2012   JC813'.54   C2011-906754-4

The Taming is a work of fiction. Names, characters, places and incidents are products of the author's imagination or are used fictitiously. Any resemblance to actual events or locales or persons, living or dead, is entirely coincidental.

Cover images: couple © Holger Winkler/A.B./Corbis, masks © Osman özdemir | Dreamstime.com, ribbon © Ekaterma Fribus | Dreamstime.com
Printed and bound in the USA

Published in Canada by Doubleday Canada,
a division of Random House of Canada Limited

Visit Random House of Canada Limited's website: www.randomhouse.ca

10 9 8 7 6 5 4 3 2 1

For Jack Toten, a gentleman in every way.

—Teresa Toten

For my daughters, Christina and Julia, who have always stood on their own two strong feet.

—Eric Walters

You may shoot me with your words,
You may cut me with your eyes,
You may kill me with your hatefulness,
But still, like air, I'll rise.

From *Still I Rise* by Maya Angelou

Chapter One

The noises in my head got louder. It was like I was a walking construction site. Metal crashed into concrete and a relentless hammering pounded "*Run, Katie, get off the stage, freak, hide, hide.*" Instead I clutched my script tighter. I was projectile sweating. I knew from auditions last week that gripping the pages with my wet hands would end up moulding my script into a rock-hard and useless bow tie. "*Cut and run, Katie. Go!*"

I focused on my most important audience member. Ms. Cooper smiled at me like I'd just discovered penicillin. "That was lovely, Katie. Nice tone and perfect clarity. I'm sure our director would agree."

Travis nodded and gave me his signature A-OK sign.

We were in the middle of our first read-through in our first script meeting. Travis hadn't taken over the reins from Ms. Cooper yet. That would happen in first rehearsals, starting tomorrow. It should have been more reassuring that the director was an actual friend. Thing is, Travis was just as surprised as I was that I got the lead. So how was he going to save me when they realized the massive mistake they'd all made when they gave me Katherina, the shrew, the lead role? It could get ugly.

Ms. Cooper flipped through her manuscript. "Katie, page thirteen of your script, please. Everybody else just pay attention to Katie's rhythm here. I want you all to think about her pitch and near-perfect feeling for the language."

Oh dear God, why would she say that? Now they were all looking and would feel compelled to hate me. Even *I* felt compelled to hate me.

I didn't unfurl my mangled *Taming of the Shrew* script. I knew the speech she meant. The rest of the cast, including Josh, my Petruchio, sat and faced me. I searched for signs of contempt and couldn't find any. It was confusing.

"Centre stage, dear. Josh, pay attention," Ms. Cooper said.

I stepped forward into the key light and prepared to respond to Ms. Cooper's reading of Petruchio's lines. Josh looked like he'd rather be performing surgery on himself. Everyone said that Josh had been tapped for the lead because of his physical presence, which, in all honesty, was significantly smouldering. I think Ms. Cooper and Travis both hoped that Josh would magically develop actor chops through rehearsals. At the moment, our dumpling-ish, five-foot-nothing, pastel-wearing drama teacher was a more convincing Petruchio than Josh was. And Josh knew it.

"Ready, Katie?" she asked.

I nodded and listened for my cue. This part was bad, the waiting for my cue part. The construction noises stopped just in time for my new obsession to take over. I scanned the stage searching for the horror-movie machinery. This was where the vat of pig's blood would tip over and drench me and my colossal actor pretentions and everyone would hoot and laugh and . . . wait a minute. *What* pretensions? I hadn't asked for the lead. I was never gunning for the part of the fiery and crazed Katherina. I was going for costumes and crowd scenes. It was Ms. Cooper who'd insisted I read for Katherina on the last day of auditions. I'd wanted to die, kill her, and blow up the school, in that order . . . until I read that first speech out loud.

Standing in the middle of the stage, under a spotlight, facing a motley audience of our future director, Travis, and Lisa, two of my best friends—okay my *only* two friends—plus a few teachers, six detention students and a couple of straggling stagehands all with their eyes trained on me, waiting . . .

And my head exploded. I *loved* it. Acting hit me like a sucker punch and I loved, loved, loved it! I was someone else, but as that someone, I was heard and I was *seen*. Invisible Katie became visible Katherina. Every nerve ending fired and I came alive. You'd think I would have choked and screwed up my speeches. But I didn't, not once. Unbelievable. I liked being up there, and it immediately became very, *very* important that I stay up there. Somehow I was more *me* on that stage than I was anywhere else. I didn't understand it, but there it was.

The first miracle was that when the cast list was posted yesterday, Katie Rosario had been picked for Shakespeare's shrew.

The second miracle was that no one laughed or rolled their eyes when the list was posted. Josh was really pissed. Not at me being picked as his Katherina, but at his being picked for Petruchio. "No offence, Katie, you're brilliant." He shook his head. "But you'll be dragging my sorry butt from one end of the stage to the other. I apologize in advance. I just needed the credit. I don't know what the hell Cooper and Travis were smoking."

The most popular boy in the entire school, a star basketball player, not only *saw* me, but he was asking forgiveness for as yet unspecified crimes. I may have been in a fog, but I was clear enough to recognize that my life had just been turned on its head.

"Don't know what you're talking about," I lied. "You'll be a perfect Petruchio, Josh."

Now Ms. Cooper was prompting me. "Anytime, Katie, starting at line 280."

"*Call you me daughter?*" I spat.

It was the speech that a furious Kàtherina throws back at her father. She knows her father doesn't love her and is only interested in getting her off his hands. I got that—just exchange my mother for Katherina's father.

Now I promise you.
You have showed a tender fatherly regard
To wish me wed to one half lunatic,
A madcap ruffian and a swearing Jack
That thinks with oaths to face the matter out.

I spaced out again for a bit while Josh fumbled for his response. He had real trouble following the language. I don't know why I *didn't*, but I didn't. Shakespeare made sense to me. From grade nine on, I'd been reading the plays in secret. I loved the way that Shakespeare's words felt on my tongue, *and* I trusted him. I got him, and now look where that had got me. What would be the price I'd have to pay for this? There was always a price.

As soon as my lines were done I was Carrie in the Stephen King movie again, the 1976 one with Sissy Spacek, not the 2002 poseur version. I'd been YouTubing the pig's blood scene ever since I got the part. Red rivers of blood stream daintily down Sissy Spacek's stunned face until it eventually obliterates her shoulders, her arms, her prom dress. Poor thing, she thought her life had changed too.

"Katie?" It was Travis, our, *my*, director. I turned to him. "Remember that by the time you get to '*I'll see thee hanged on Sunday first*' you have to have established yourself as loud, crude. Katherina is a wild animal that has to be tamed. Give Petruchio something to tame."

Josh turned a paler shade of grey.

"Don't let this 'tameness' be your Achilles' heel, Katie," Ms. Cooper interrupted. "You are rage and power personified, you—"

"Will love it," I whispered.

"Pardon, dear?" asked Ms. Cooper, who kept forgetting that she was not the director.

"Nothing, excuse me." I turned to Travis. "I'm ready to peel wallpaper, sir."

Travis nodded, pleased with himself and, more importantly, with me. Travis *saw* me. He usually did, but now, because he was a director and I was on stage, everybody looked. Everybody saw me. And somehow, in the seeing, the horror-movie machinery dissolved. There was just me, and everybody looking at me.

I'd spent a lot of time and a whole lot of effort trying to blend into the walls in my last couple of schools. Being invisible kept me safe in the hallways *and* with the last two of Mom's boyfriends. But that was over now. I was starring in *The Taming of the Shrew* and it hit me that, at least on opening night, just about everyone in the school would see me. And, sweating on stage, waiting for Josh to recover his lines, it also hit me that being invisible was good, but maybe now being *visible* was going to be better . . . so, so, so much better.

Chapter Two

❦

"I'll prompt you," Lisa said. "Wherever in the script you need or want. No probs."

We were standing on the dark and empty stage, by ourselves. Everyone had gone home long ago.

"I mean it. I memorized the whole thing." Lisa jumped down and plunked herself into a seat in the second row, right behind the place where Travis always sat.

"What?! You did what?"

"Oh, get over yourself." I could barely see her. "You know I do that sort of thing without breaking a sweat." She threw her legs over the back of the chair in front of her. "You also know that this school bores the snot out of me—almost as much as the other schools." Lisa sighed dramatically in the soupy darkness. "It's just that, for better or worse, I have you and Travis here. And you two dickheads are deep into this Stratford fantasy of yours, so . . . I offer you both my services." She crossed her arms. Or I think she did, it was hard to tell, even squinting.

"Go ahead, Olivier, pick something!"

"Olivier was a *male* actor," I pointed out.

"Yeah, but he was the best, right?"

I wanted to be sure of something. I walked over to a stool at stage right and inhaled the auditorium, the velvet quiet. I didn't need or want to review anything as much as I wanted to check to see if what I had felt was real. Up here, right now, it was real. *I was real.* And it felt good.

"Something happens to you up there and it's nuclear," Lisa said. "Even I wouldn't have believed it unless I'd seen it for myself, and I worship your dainty size-nines. There is more to you than meets the eye, Katie Rosario."

"Shakespeare?" I asked.

"*Pirates of the Caribbean.*"

"Same diff," we both said at once. Friends did that, said stupid, ordinary stuff like that at the same time, and Lisa was my friend. For years, I'd driven strictly by myself. From the beginning of middle school on, it was easier to be uncluttered, cleaner, not needing anybody. And that was good.

But this was better.

Travis and Lisa, my gang, my group, smartest thing I'd ever done. They loved the girl they thought they knew. And I loved them right back. As best I could.

Lisa stood up. "Give me lines 154 to 160 in the capitulation speech at the end. She's tamed, drunk the Kool-Aid, Petruchio is her prince and she's going to behave."

I had to search for several minutes. Unlike Lisa, I hadn't even committed my part, let alone the entire play, to memory.

"Remember how adorable 'His Hotness,' your Petruchio, is, if that helps."

"Poor Josh!" we both said.

I turned to the stool and saw my prince.

Too little payment for so great a debt.
Such duty as the subject oweth to her husband.
And not obedient to his honest will,

What is she but a foul contending rebel
And graceless traitor to her loving lord?
I am ashamed that women are so simple.

And then Lisa clapped, and I believed me. Not as Katie, of course, but I believed that as Katherina I would find myself a "loving lord," and if I believed it, I could make anyone believe it. Yup, pathetic little Katie Rosario could do all this and more. Lisa was still clapping. And I was sure.

Chapter Three

I drove up to the school. There were lots of cars inching along the road, and as I turned into the driveway I was almost forced to stop to avoid hitting students walking along the sidewalk. Moving slower I drove through the parking lot, looking for a space, avoiding cars dropping kids off. The last thing I wanted to do was start my first day with a fender-bender. First impressions matter, and that wasn't the one I wanted to make.

It looked like there wasn't a spot left anywhere. I should have got here earlier. I was cutting it way too close. A late slip wouldn't be as bad as a traffic accident, but still, not the best start, and—there was a place!

I cranked the wheel and pulled the car into the empty spot. I turned the mirror to check out my hair—it looked good . . . really good— and then straightened my tie. Everything was good. I climbed out.

I knew I had to report to the office. I just didn't know where the office was. Or even how to get into the school. There were double doors at the end of the parking lot. I walked over and tried one—it was locked. I pulled the second door. It was locked too. A guy pushed open the door from the inside.

"Thank you," I said.

"No problem. You a supply teacher?" he asked.

"No, I'm a new student. Why would you think I was a teacher?"

"A *supply* teacher. I know all the actual teachers here."

"Why would you think I was *any* sort of teacher?"

"That car you drove in with. Students don't usually drive high-end Audis."

"And teachers here do?"

He snorted. "Not usually, but teacher's still a safer bet than student. And you're not dressed like a student either." He gestured towards my tie and jacket.

"Oh . . . this . . . I just didn't know . . . isn't there any dress code here?"

"Yeah, but it says basically no bandanas, nothing with swear words, don't show too much skin—nothing about wearing a jacket and tie."

I was just so used to having to dress up for school that it never occurred to me it would be different here at a public school, but of course it was.

"Just trying to make a good impression," I said.

"You dress like that and you'll make an *impression*, but I don't think it will be so good."

I almost said something about the way he was dressed—like he'd rolled a drunk and stolen his clothes—but I didn't. No point in alienating somebody in the first minute of my first day. Besides, he was probably right.

I took off the jacket and started to pull off the tie when the bell rang.

"Great . . . first day and I'm already late," I said.

"That's first bell. You still have five minutes to get to class," he said. "Where is your first class?"

"Actually I don't know yet. I'm supposed to report to the office . . . I don't even know where that is."

"Go up those stairs," he said, pointing down a corridor. "One flight up and turn to your right. You can't miss it."

"Thanks." I paused. "Could you do me a favour?"

"Depends on the favour."

"I don't want to carry these around and I don't have a locker to put them in and I need to get to the office fast. Could you just put them in my car for me?" I held out the keys. "You can give me back the keys at lunch. I'll meet you in the cafeteria . . . lunch can be on me." It would be good to have somebody to eat with the first day.

"Sure, I can do that," he said.

I handed him the clothes and the keys. He held the keys up. "Do you always go around handing the keys to a fifty-thousand-dollar car to perfect strangers?"

"Come on, you can't really be perfect, can you?" I joked.

"Depends on who you ask. There are a couple of teachers here who think I'm a perfect idiot. But still, aren't you afraid I'll just take off?"

"I have insurance for car theft."

"How about if I just take it out for a joyride?" he asked.

I shrugged. "Be my guest. There's a full tank. Just make sure you find a parking spot, and don't change the settings on my sound system."

He laughed. "And if I banged it up a little?"

"My insurance also covers collision and damage. No sweat."

At least it was no sweat for me. My father might have had a different opinion, but I really didn't care that much what he thought—it wasn't like his opinion of me could get much worse.

"By the way," he said, "I'm Danny."

"Evan," I said, holding out my hand to shake.

He looked surprised. What was he expecting, a fist-bump, a high-five, a hug? He shifted the clothes into his other hand and we awkwardly shook.

"Pleased to meet you," I said.

"Yeah, real pleasure," he said. There was a smirk on his face.

"I'll see you at lunch, and thanks, man."

"No problem. Thanks for the *car*. With any luck I should be back from my joyride by lunch," he said.

He was looking for my reaction. I wasn't going to give him one—well, at least not the one he expected.

"Like I said, as long as you don't screw around with the sound system, that works for me. See you later."

I caught a glimpse of his expression—surprise, maybe even a little bit of shock—before I turned and headed in the direction of the office.

I got up from the seat against the wall and walked over to the counter.

"Excuse me," I called out to the secretary, "isn't the headmaster free yet?"

"Headmaster?" She looked as though I'd said something amusing. "Do you mean the *principal*?"

"Yes, yes, the principal. I've been waiting almost an hour."

"He's very busy and—" She stopped as the door with "Principal" on it opened, and we both turned. Two students—younger than me—came out, followed by a man who I assumed was the head . . . the principal. None of them looked too happy.

"I think he might be free now," she said. "Mr. Waldman!" she called out. "Your eight-thirty appointment is here."

"Show him in." He retreated back into his office.

I walked around the edge of the counter and pushed open a little swinging door. I stopped at the threshold of the principal's office.

He sat there behind his desk, partially hidden by a pile of folders, head down, working. I knocked on the door frame.

He looked up. "Come in . . . please."

"Hello, my name is Evan Campbell." I reached out my hand. "I'm pleased to meet you, sir."

He looked as surprised as Danny had, but reacted more quickly. He stood partway up and we shook hands. His grip was weak—my father said that you could tell a lot about a man from the way he shook hands. Weak grip, weak person.

"I'm glad to meet you, as well. I always try to get to know all the students in the school."

"How many students are in this school, sir?"

"Fifteen . . . no, closer to sixteen hundred."

I was pretty sure that if he didn't even know the *number* of students he definitely didn't know the *individual* students. Again, that worked well for me. It would be easier to disappear into the masses, and my plan was to blend in, cause no problems, graduate and get back to my life the way it was *supposed* to go. In nine months this school would be nothing more than an unpleasant memory.

"Actually, come to think of it, enrolment is up this year so I guess we're creeping closer to seventeen hundred students," the principal said.

"My last school only had two hundred students, with an average class size of ten."

"Not something that will ever happen here." I guessed that was pointing out the obvious. Now he was frowning. "When this appointment was made I assumed your parents would come in with you."

"My father is somewhere over the Pacific Ocean. He's on a business trip to Japan, sir."

"There's no need to call me sir," he said.

"My parents always insist that I show respect to adults, sir, but especially to those who are my teachers."

"Well, good manners are always appreciated, I'm sure . . . And your mother?"

"My mother has a board meeting today. She's very active with charitable causes. Today is East General Hospital, I believe. My mother was here when I registered last week, sir," I replied. "I just thought that it would be appropriate to meet with you today, to introduce myself to my principal."

That was a lie. My father thought it was what I was supposed to do—introduce myself to the headmaster. I assumed his assistant had made this appointment, since he wouldn't have had time for that.

"That was very considerate of you. It shows good manners . . . good breeding."

"Thank you," I said. My father would have loved the "good breeding" comment.

"I had my secretary flag your student record when it arrived," he went on. "The files came in yesterday."

Great. Just what I needed. I was here to leave that history behind and now it was following me.

He fumbled around on his desk, shuffling papers and folders and files till he found my records and started reading. "You have certainly been in a lot of schools."

I could tell he was counting, his head down, finger running down the page. I could have saved him some time by telling him the number, but I didn't.

"Eleven," he finally said.

"My father's career has necessitated a number of moves, sir."

"In a number of countries. Japan . . . Germany . . . and is this one in Luxembourg?"

"We lived there for almost eighteen months. It was a very nice school."

"I imagine it would be. These are all private schools, are they not? But now . . . this school . . . this *isn't* a private school."

I tried not to laugh. My little walk through the halls and my time spent waiting in the office had shown me just how *not* a private school this was.

"Why did you register so suddenly, and now, almost two weeks into the school year?" he asked.

Obviously that reason *wasn't* included in my student record. I was pleased, relieved, but not really surprised. I didn't suppose the headmaster, or the teachers involved, would have wanted to risk a lawsuit by going on record with why I was asked to leave my last school.

I took a deep breath. I'd been rehearsing this line.

"I feel badly talking about it," I said. "This is difficult." I looked down at my feet. I knew how to fake upset and shame. I could play almost any role. "My tuition was expensive . . . there were some problems . . . the recession . . . financial setbacks . . ."

"I understand," he said. "No need to say anything more."

Actually I hadn't really said anything, so I hadn't really lied. In truth, my father had more money than God, but it wasn't like he'd be talking to my father. He wasn't coming to this school any more than he'd come to any of my others. And I figured there wasn't much chance of the two of them just running into each other . . . it wasn't like this guy ran in the same social circles as my parents.

"I think you'll find some things are very different at our school," Mr. Waldman said.

"I'm sure there will be differences, but I've heard this is a very fine school," I said.

"Yes . . . yes, it is." He didn't sound very confident in that statement. Instead, he looked somewhat taken aback, surprised. Apparently, even *he* didn't believe this was a fine school.

"And really, sir," I continued, "a school is only a building. It's the staff of a school that makes it a good institution of learning."

"That is certainly correct," he agreed, although he didn't say it with any confidence or tell me how "wonderful" his staff was. "I just hope the curriculum here will be challenging enough. I've been led to believe that private schools often provide a more *stringent* curriculum than the public system."

"I'm not sure if they were more stringent, sir . . . perhaps just different. There are some areas where I might be more advanced, but others where I'm sure I'll have to work especially hard to make up lost ground. Thank you for your time, sir."

He smiled and then stood up, and I did the same, getting to my feet quickly. He extended his hand and we shook again. This time his grip was much more firm. I turned, walked out and closed the door behind me. I didn't need to think twice to know that I'd impressed him. Stupid people were easy to impress.

Chapter Four

I flowed along with the crowd of people moving from their period one to period two classes. There wasn't a lot of order. Actually, there was no order at all unless you counted size—big people moved littler people out of their way unless they moved first. Students rushed noisily, bumping along with no proper sense of decorum. If any of this was an example of the behaviour in this school, there wasn't going to be much that I could do that would get me into trouble. Sometimes the key wasn't to try harder but to simply lower the standards. It was like hanging around with fat people so you look thin. Here I'd be practically anorexic, or at least compared to these people, a star.

I looked down at my sheet again—Drama, Room 273, Ms. Cooper. Room 273 was right ahead, the door was open and I walked in. The chairs were arranged in a large circle with a big opening in the middle. Already some of the seats were taken and there was a group talking and laughing in the corner. There was no sign of any teacher. I didn't know if I should just sit down or if there were assigned seats. Awkwardly I stood beside the teacher's desk at the front of the room. I'd have to wait, but standing there while people filed in was just plain wrong—anxious and unsure of myself was not the image I was going for. It was hard enough to be new but worse standing up there like I was on display. I just wanted this Ms. Cooper to arrive so I could sit down and blend into the—

"Hi, how's it going?"

I turned. It was one of the students from the group in the corner. She was dressed in a mismatch of floaty colours and clothing and she was wearing sandals—with socks! Why was it that the *pretty* and *popular* girls never came up to say hello without asking? Then again, they didn't *need* to.

"Fine. It's going fine," I answered. I hoped she'd just go away.

"Good. You're new."

"First day." I wouldn't be unfriendly but I certainly wasn't going to be friendly.

"I hope people are making you feel welcome," she said.

"So far people have been very friendly and helpful."

"Good to hear. Class should start soon," she said. "Just take a seat."

"I will. I just want to let the teacher know that I'm here."

She gave me a confused look. "The teacher *does* know you're here."

"Well, I'd like to talk to her."

She then turned to the other students. "This gentleman is waiting to talk to Ms. Cooper before he sits down."

There was a murmur of comments and giggling. Didn't anybody in this school have any manners? And who was she with her sandals and socks trying to give me a hard time? I was just trying to do the right thing and—she reached out and took my timetable.

"Well, hello, Evan Campbell. Glad you're here." She paused. "And by the way, I'm Ms. Cooper . . . your teacher."

I felt a rush of heat signalling embarrassment and anger.

"What confused you?" she asked. "Was it my cutting-edge fashion sense, my youthful appearance or my casual and sarcastic attitude?"

"I think it was all three of those things," I said. Now, I'd have to pour on the charm to make up for my misstep.

"Obviously a very bright young man. Bright *and* perceptive enough to suck up to his new teacher. Now, here's your timetable. Just take a seat anywhere."

I took back my timetable and slowly walked across the room, trying to move confidently, calmly. I knew everybody was looking at me, but that was okay. I wasn't making *that* bad a first impression, even if I hadn't realized the teacher was a teacher.

A big knot of people came barging in through the door, noisy and unruly—and the bell rang out. They filtered in and sat down until there were only a few empty seats—one on each side of me. Way to make me feel welcome.

I looked around the circle at a mishmash of people, dressed in a dozen different styles, or lack of styles, including some guy with heavy black makeup. Certainly nothing like the crisp conformity of school uniforms I was used to. I knew this drill, being the new kid. I knew it too well, having played it too often. I was going for cool and detached. The best way to fit in was to act like you didn't *need* to fit in.

Equally different were the faces. In my old schools there had always been a couple of Chinese kids and an occasional African kid whose father was on a diplomatic mission, but they'd stood out in a sea of faces so white they looked like a blanket of new-fallen snow. Here I was pretty much in the minority. I guess, actually, *everybody* was in the minority. Black, Asian, brown and white . . . interestingly they weren't sitting in any perceivable pattern. They were sort of mixed up. In all of my old schools the few "ethnic" kids usually clustered together—maybe because they shared a language or culture. Maybe, though, they sat together just for safety—at least for emotional safety. It wasn't as if anybody was going to hit them. Violence wasn't something that lurked in the hallowed halls of the schools that I'd attended. I wasn't so sure that was the case here.

"Okay, let's get settled in and start being dramatic!" Ms. Cooper called out.

The noise level settled down and she walked into the centre of the circle.

"'A classic is a book which people praise and don't read,'" Ms. Cooper said. "Does anybody know who said that?"

Who *didn't* know who said that?

Nobody's hand went up. Were they just being unco-operative, or did nobody actually know the answer?

"Anybody . . . come on. Somebody has to know," she prodded.

Again, no response. It was now obvious that nobody knew.

"How about if I sweeten the pot. If anybody can guess the right answer it will be worth five marks, and I'll dismiss the class early so you can have an extra-long lunch."

Kids sat up straighter in their seats. She now had their attention, but she still didn't have anybody volunteering an answer. Bribes can't produce answers if the answers aren't there.

"Come on, *somebody* make a guess," one of the students pleaded.

"Tell you what," Ms. Cooper said, "I'll give you *three* guesses, so make sure you make them good ones."

"William Shakespeare!" one of the girls yelled out.

"Great guess!" Ms. Cooper exclaimed, and the kids burst into applause. "But wrong." That silenced the applause.

"Dr. Seuss?" one of the boys joked.

"Wrong again. And that's two guesses."

The class collectively groaned.

"I was just joking!" he protested.

"Too bad. A guess is a guess," she said. "You'd better think about this, talk it over before you make any more bad guesses or–"

"Samuel Clements," I said.

"No!" somebody screamed out. "No more guesses!"

Ms. Cooper smiled. "Do people want it to count?"

"Is he right?" that same girl asked.

Ms. Cooper just gave a bigger smile in response. "I'm not telling you if he's right or wrong. You have to decide as a class: do you trust your new classmate?" She turned to look at me, as did every eye in the room.

"I'm right." I said it confidently. I *was* right.

"Has anybody even heard of Samuel . . . Samuel . . . whatever he said?" the Emo-boy asked.

"Clements," Ms. Cooper said.

There was more mumbled conversation as people were trying to come to some decision.

"It's the right answer." I paused. "Trust me." I flashed my best smile.

"I believe him," a girl said—a very pretty girl. "I say we trust him."

I did have a way of getting pretty girls to trust me . . . at least in the beginning.

"That would be wise," Ms. Cooper said. "It *is* in fact Samuel Clements, a.k.a. Mark Twain. Thanks to Evan, we will be dismissed early for lunch!"

There were cheers and hoots, and the guy two seats away leaned over and slapped me on the back.

"But first let's accomplish a little bit of work. We are going to start reading one of the classics. It was written by arguably the greatest writer in the history of the English language."

Oh, great, we were going to be reading *Romeo and Juliet* or *Hamlet* or–

The door opened. It was Danny!

"Good morning, or is it already afternoon?" Ms. Cooper said.

"Come on, I'm only slightly late," Danny said.

"Slightly was over fifteen minutes ago. You know the rules. You have to provide either a valid and truthful reason for your tardiness, or perform a dramatically told, yet believable story, or you have to go to the office for a late slip." Ms. Cooper gestured for him to come into the centre of the circle and she retreated off to the side.

"Okay, here's my reason. I was heading outside for a smoke this morning and I ran into this guy, this guy I'd never even *met*, and he just handed me the keys to his car . . . an Audi TT . . . and he asked if I could drop something off in the car and return the keys to him later."

"So far, what's the opinion of the audience . . . the judges . . . is he telling the truth, or at least providing a credible lie?" Ms. Cooper asked.

People all around the circle, almost without exception, gave him two thumbs down. I didn't do anything.

"Tough room. I'll continue," Danny said. "But this guy, he said that if I wanted I could even take his car for a little spin, and I wasn't going to, but it *was* an Audi and I've never even sat in an Audi, so I took it for a ride."

I couldn't help but wince in reaction.

"And man, you wouldn't *believe* just how fast that car can go and how well it corners and—"

"I think that's about enough. Raise your hand if you think he's lying?" Ms. Cooper asked.

Every hand went up but mine.

"I guess it's unanimous . . . except for Evan." She paused. "Evan, do you actually believe his story?"

"Well . . ."

"Could I at least *finish* my story?" Danny protested. He reached into his pocket and pulled out keys—*my* keys. "Here, Evan," he said, and he tossed them to me.

"That story is true?" Ms. Cooper gasped.

Danny gracefully bowed from the waist. Ms. Cooper started to clap, and then the rest of the class jumped to their feet and began clapping and cheering.

"I think there is no point in us trying to top that dramatic presentation!" Ms. Cooper called out above the noise. "And because of that you are all dismissed—now—for a very, *very* early lunch!"

The cheering got even louder.

"But remember, I'll see you all tonight, right after school, in the auditorium . . . 3:30 sharp, and no excuses from anybody!"

Chapter Five

❦

The thrill for the day, probably even the year, was that we got a new guy in drama, a senior. It was a major topic of conversation in the cafeteria at lunch. Ms. Cooper's class was pretty well divided between grade elevens and twelves, and the girls in our class went hormonal when they got within spitting distance of a male who showers. It was a nuclear blowback when Evan Campbell stepped into Room 273. Not that you'd have caught me looking. I didn't play that game. What was the point?

But God, he was over six feet worth of wow. *And* apparently smart, too. *And* . . . he drove an Audi! I'd spent the rest of the period looking, but not looking. Evan Campbell was yummy. Wait, who thought that thought? That wasn't me. I didn't think thoughts like that. This was where being invisible came in handy. No one could see me thinking thoughts that weren't like my thoughts, and he certainly wouldn't have even known I was in the room. I absolutely did not react to boys like that. And he was just another boy. But not.

I'd concentrated on Ms. Cooper with renewed intensity. She was my version of a cold shower. Then Danny entered with that too-stupid-to-be-true true story.

I couldn't wait to tell Lisa. I mean, an Audi! Of course that in itself wouldn't have impressed Lisa. Her parents had major money, and they would have bought her an Audi, or a small country, if she'd just promised to stay in therapy.

"My, my, what a wonder to behold," Travis said as he plopped onto a seat at my table in the cafeteria.

"What's a wonder?" I asked.

"The new guy . . . the one you're staring at from across the room."

"I'm not staring at anybody," I said, as I stopped eyeballing Evan.

"Lie to me if you want, honey, but don't lie to yourself," Travis sighed.

Hey, it was the eighth wonder of the world that I had any friends, period. I sucked at the bonding stuff at the best of times. Yet Travis had been my best friend from the moment I came to the school last year in grade ten. He'd picked me out even as I was trying to blend into the lockers and even though he was a year ahead of me. We found Lisa three weeks before Christmas. Also new to the school, Lisa came from a number of places, the most recent being a boarding school called Rigby College. She'd had enough with the wilderness of Port Henry and the aggressive idiocy of entitled trust fund kids. She liked me and Travis better, way better. Go figure. So by early December of last year, I had a "group" and guaranteed survivability. It had been a long time since I'd had either. It took some getting used to.

Lisa joined me and Travis that day for a late lunch in the cafeteria, which was not so affectionately known as the Droopy Diaper Café. I wasn't sure but I thought the smell of the place had a lot to do with the name. Even in the soup of what passes for your modern urban high school student body, my friends were noticeable. I was their beige-on-beige wallpaper; they stood out even more with me as their backdrop. Although Travis and Lisa would have hotly denied it, the two of them were as much "in uniform" as our site-specific crop of nerds, goths, preps, orange fashionistas, druggies, gangstas, band kids, jocks, players and that whole shambling army of kids called the silent majority. That's probably where I would have belonged, except even *they* were too visible for me.

Travis doled out our lunches. It was his turn to wait in line. There was macaroni and french fries for him, and organic mystery meat for Lisa and me. Travis had been Emo-boy since grade nine. Danny—sitting across the way with Josh and Evan—liked to point out, on a daily basis, that "Emo is over," but Travis insisted, on the same daily basis, that he was going to single-handedly revive the movement, skinny jeans, swept hair, foo-foo music and all.

Lisa was a different story altogether. She was barely civil. Somehow that added to her allure. Lisa's "tell it like it is" method of communication had earned her respect and a fair bit of fear from her immediate peer group, us. I personally thought she slid some-where onto the Asperger's scale, but her folks had therapied her into what passed for almost normal. The other thing that got her respect was that she was smarter than anyone else in the school, including the teachers, and the teachers knew it. Lisa's "uniform" consisted of some combination of a "this season" skirt her mother brought back from Bloomingdale's mixed in with something from the Goodwill slush pile. Travis finished off Lisa's look by colouring her hair a deep burgundy with brilliant fuchsia in alternating sections.

Uniforms aside, Lisa's best feature, like Travis's, was that she liked me. This year I'd really tried to accept that. Like I said, I didn't "do friends" at the other schools. This was weird, but good weird.

I was probably smiling vacantly at the two of them as I tried to drown out Mom's voice, which was Velcroed in my brain all day. Lisa called it my "middle-distance" look, the one immortalized by a hundred million girls' junior fiction novels where the plucky heroine on the cover is looking stupidly into pretty much nowhere. Lisa said my stupid look intrigued her. She said she wanted to know where I go.

Trust me, she didn't. I went to a lot of places, but lately, I'd been going to Mom with a can of hairspray in one hand and a scotch in the other. She's smoking and spraying and she's angry.

"You think it's easy being a single mother when your kid keeps scaring off any half-decent prospect that comes sniffing around? Not this time!" She stubs out the butt like it has offended her and lights a fresh one. "When I say make yourself scarce in the evenings, I mean make yourself *God damned* scarce! We don't want to see you, Katie. Joey is the real deal, I don't want to scare off another one!"

"Our little girl is growing up," Travis said to Lisa.

"What, puberty has finally struck?" She winked at me.

"No, no, no!" Travis said. "This is all *so* exciting. Now I know how a mother bird feels when its baby wants to leave the nest. Our child has developed herself a little crush on the new boy."

"The new boy? Word is out all over the school, seriously hot. Is he here?" Lisa asked. "Can I see him?"

"Could you both just shut up . . . and sit down . . . *please*?"

Lisa looked like she was going to resist, but she must have sensed how embarrassed I felt.

"Well, is he here in the café?" she asked.

"Over there," Travis said. "With Josh and Danny."

"Lordy, is that him? That's got to be him." Lisa elbowed me and let out a low, slow whistle at the same time.

"I rest my case," said Travis, mumbling through a mouthful of macaroni.

"Okay." She narrowed her eyes. "More than standard pretty, I'll grant you. And definitely top-drawer private school type. What's he doing in this hellhole?"

"Excuse *me!*" Travis flicked a noodle at her. "You're in this hellhole too!"

"Completely different," Lisa sniffed. "I made a conscious, classic, iconoclastic choice to be here." She joined me and every other girl in the Droopy Diaper in locking on to Evan. "He, on the other hand, has a story. And I bet it's a good one."

He seemed to be having a great time horsing around with Danny and Josh. And I had a great time looking. Evan was like nothing and no one I had ever seen before. And, a handy little bonus of being invisible, I could look all I wanted and no one could see me looking.

Chapter Six

I balanced my tray as we moved across the cafeteria. Judging by the smell this was just one more way in which my present school couldn't hope to measure up to any of my previous schools. There was an aroma suggesting a fast food restaurant . . . correction, the dumpster behind a fast food restaurant.

"We always sit here," Danny said as he settled at an empty table in the corner.

I sat down two seats from him.

"By the way," he said, "I didn't really take your car for a drive. That part was a lie. I'm just always late for class. I think they'd be surprised if I was on time."

"That was a very believable lie," I said. "But you could have taken the car if you'd wanted."

"I might just take you up on that. How about as a first step you drive me home after the drama practice tonight?"

"Can I take a rain check? I'm going to leave right at the bell."

"Well, I guess you could do that . . . if you want to fail drama," he said.

I gave him a questioning look.

"Apparently you don't know that doing something in the school play is part of the drama course—you get marked for it."

"You're joking, right?"

"I wish I was. But no worries, all the roles have been cast so you'll be backstage crew. Most of the time we just sit around and shoot the crap."

I would actually have preferred to be in the play, not doing some donkey work behind the scenes. I didn't mind being on stage . . . no, I actually *liked* it, and if I'd been around when the roles were cast I was sure I probably would have been the lead.

"What play are we doing?" I asked.

"A classic by none other than that Willie Shakespeare guy."

"Let me guess," I said. "It has to be *Romeo and Juliet* or *Hamlet*, or maybe *Macbeth*."

"No, no and, um, no."

"So what play are we doing?"

"*The Taming of the Shrew*," Danny replied.

"*That* would not have been my guess."

"I sort of noticed." He laughed. "And right now you're about to meet the proud actor in the lead role, Petractlio."

"That would be Petruchio, unless you're doing a very, *very* different version," I said.

"You even know the names of the characters?" Danny asked in amazement.

"The main characters."

"Hey, Pistachio!" Danny called out. "How you doing, you nut?"

The guy put down his tray and then slid into a seat at our table. He was tall and looked athletic—more like a jock than a drama geek.

"Josh, this is Evan. Evan, this is Josh."

I started to get to my feet to shake hands but remembered that wasn't done around here.

"Good to meet you, man," he said.

"You too."

"I was just telling Evan about his involvement in the school play," Danny said. "How it's mandatory."

"Yeah, part of the course. Of course I didn't think me getting the lead role was gonna be part of it." He held up his hands. "Look, my palms get sweaty just talking about getting in front of an audience."

Danny laughed. "I figured that wouldn't bother you. You've played in front of large groups before."

"Big difference between performing on a stage and being on a basketball court," he said.

He *was* an athlete. That made sense. I liked when things made sense. I'd rather have been able to predict something bad than not see something good coming . . . wow, that was strange. It was just that it was safer to be able to predict things. If you tripped and gravity didn't make you fall, it would be less painful than hitting the ground but way too strange.

"Five hundred people in an auditorium should be nothing after screaming crowds in the stands."

"Big difference. I sort of know what I'm doing on the basketball court."

"Look who's being modest," Danny said. He turned to me. "Josh here is the school's star athlete. How many scholarships have you been offered for university next year?"

"More than a few," he said. "And absolutely *none* for acting."

"Well, that's not surprising," Danny said. "I mean, I've seen how the rehearsals are going."

"Thanks for the vote of confidence," Josh said.

"I'm only telling you what you already know, right?"

"No argument," he said.

"Don't take this the wrong way, but I'm not even sure why Cooper gave you the lead."

"You're not the only one," Josh agreed. "Ms. Cooper said something about how she wanted to *stretch* me. If she was going to stretch me a couple more inches it would at least help with my rebound stats."

"Maybe Cooper was just thinking that you being in the play would bring in the ladies, guaranteed," Danny said.

"Yeah, like that's gonna work. I'm afraid the sight of me in tights isn't gonna be anyone's idea of fun. Why couldn't she just let me play ball?" He turned to me. "Do you play ball?"

"Technically, but not basketball. Rugby."

"Rugby, now that's a sport!" Josh said. "Football without equipment. You have to be either fearless or stupid to play that sport!"

"It helps if you're a bit of both," I said.

"I don't know," Danny said. "I think I have the stupid part of it down so I should be a great rugby player. But I'd rather play football, or rugby or have people throw axes at my head than play the lead in *The Taming of the Shrew.*"

"Thanks a lot, I appreciate your ongoing support," Josh said.

"Come on, just having some fun—at your expense."

"So . . . who's playing Katherina?" I asked.

"Katie, Katie Rosario," Josh said. "Now *that* was a surprise, too!"

"Yeah, but there is one big difference between her playing Katherina and you playing Pinocchio," Danny said.

"It's Petruchio, not Pinocchio," I said, correcting him.

"Not the way he plays it," Danny said. "He's made of wood and trying to be a real boy. But the difference is that Katie is doing a really great job."

"I can always count on you for kind words," Josh said. "I never would have guessed it either, but she's awesome."

These two were probably easy to impress. Simple minds amused by simple things. I nodded along.

"That's the part that surprised me the most," Danny said. "She's usually so quiet that you don't even notice her, but up there on the stage . . . she's . . . she's *different*."

"Yeah she even *looks* different," Josh said. "Okay, now this is going to sound strange."

"Look who you're talking to," Danny said. "I *like* strange."

"It's just that . . . well . . . you know, when she walks around the school, she's okay looking, even cute, but once she gets on stage . . . well . . ."

"It's like you can't take your eyes off her," Danny said.

"I thought it was only me!" Josh actually looked a little embarrassed.

"Nope, me too. It's like she changes before your eyes. The only reason nobody's noticed I'm staring at her is because everybody else is staring too," Danny said.

"She's going to be incredible," Josh said, "which, of course, only makes me look worse by comparison."

"Maybe her talent will rub off on you."

"I'm not counting big on that."

"Now I'm curious," I said. "I guess I'll see her for myself at the rehearsal tonight."

"You've actually seen her already," Danny said. "She's in our drama class."

"She is?"

"She might even be in the cafeteria now," Josh suggested. He stood up and looked around. "There she is!"

I turned around and half stood so I could see, but I couldn't tell who he was pointing at.

"The table at the side . . . where there are a bunch of girls and Travis . . . she's wearing a blue top."

"There are lots of tables with lots of girls and lots of people in blue, and who's Travis?" I asked.

Without answering, Josh stood on his chair and then climbed up onto the table. "Katherina!" he yelled out, waving his arms above his head.

Chapter Seven

In a single bound, as they say, Josh leapt onto a cafeteria chair and, horror of Stephen King horrors, called out to me. Or to Katherina, to be more precise.

"It is I, your husband to be, Petruchio!" Josh yelled. "Kate . . . *Pluck up your spirits! Look cheerfully upon me!*" It looked like the new guy was feeding him lines, without a book.

"That's not bad," Travis snorted. "The best I've heard from him yet. Maybe we should do the play in the cafeteria instead of the auditorium." He crossed his arms and his eyes. "Hmmm . . . he's supposed to be so fearless on the court. How about we go to a game?"

"Over your dead body," Lisa groaned. "Look, Josh is in his element here, with an ever-adoring cafeteria crowd and someone feeding him lines. That boy is going to suck on a proper stage no matter what you do."

Josh, followed by Danny and Evan, stood up and—worse, way worse—headed our way.

Oh. Dear. God. You could actually hear "*He means Katie Rosario,*" in whispered waves breaking throughout the cafeteria. I responded with my new thing, championship sweating.

Josh continued towards me, stepping from chair to chair and then right onto our table! He didn't seem to be worried about people staring at him.

"Kate, dear Kate." Josh bowed elaborately. "I apologize, ahead of time, for making tonight's rehearsal unbearable for you and everyone else! Forgive me, dear, dear shrew!" The Droopy Diaper was riveted.

"Don't worry," Lisa muttered. "There aren't two of them that know what the hell a shrew is." She raised an eyebrow. "Are you perspiring?" she whispered.

I answered by pinning both my arms to my sides.

Josh extended his hand towards me.

"Can you get down from the table?" I asked. "*Please?* . . . It's sort of embarrassing."

"I will, fair Kate, if you will agree that Sunday is our wedding day!" he bellowed.

By now everybody in the whole cafeteria had stopped eating and talking and was gawking and laughing. It was pretty hilarious— at least, it would have been if it had been anybody but me.

"Come down, *please,*" I said.

"*Nay, come Kate, come* up. *You must not look so sour!*"

I reached up and grabbed Josh's hand and pulled him down from the table while still managing to keep my underarms glued tight.

"Oh her touch is so sweet!" Josh called out as he climbed down.

The cafeteria erupted into applause.

Josh took a big bow and waved to the audience. Josh Lumsden seemed comfortable being the centre of attention everywhere except on a stage. If I was invisible, he was a gigantic flashing neon sign.

"Katie, we want you to meet somebody. This is Evan, he's new."

Lisa stuck her elbow in my side. "Ow! I mean, yeah, I know, he's in our drama class."

Evan offered me his hand. Who does that? "Pleased to meet you," he said.

"Yeah, me too," I said, or maybe I just thought it.

"I'm sorry for the embarrassment," he said. "It's all my fault. I just asked them who was playing Katherina to Josh's Petruchio."

"Well, yes, uh, because of a series of unfortunate events, that would be me."

"Lemony Snicket!" He smiled. I died.

"They say you're doing a great job."

"I'm trying." Surely that came out loud?

"I guess I'll find that out for myself after school. I was just told that I'm part of the backstage production," he said.

"I wish I were backstage."

"I'm glad you're *on* the stage," Josh offered.

"As is everybody," Travis agreed.

"Emo-boy here is the director," Danny said.

"At your service." Travis bowed.

"Be careful, Evan, it looks like Travis has a crush on you," Danny said.

"Jealous?" Travis winked.

I tried not to blush.

"Still trying to convince everyone you're queer? You can't have it both ways, you know." This was Danny's version of good-natured bantering. The shocking thing was that was just how Travis took it.

"Don't know why. Besides, sweetie," Travis batted his heavily mascaraed lashes at Danny, "you know if I were queer, I'd do you first."

"Promises, promises," Danny snorted. "I still can't believe they made you the director. Just because you wear eye makeup doesn't make you creative. Just creepy."

"Please, Danny-boy, let's not have a lovers' spat in front of everybody." Travis fussed with his hair.

Danny looked pissed. I'd seen that look before and knew where this could lead. Was he going to take a swing at Travis or—he started to laugh. They *all* started to laugh.

Guys. I'd never understand guys. Well . . . girls either. I didn't get it, but I didn't get a lot of what passed for normal teen social interaction.

"Well, it's all Greek to me." Josh shrugged. "I don't know how Travis got the director's job, or whether Cooper suffered a stroke when she cast me in the lead. I'm just glad that you're there, Katie, because you're going to be so brilliant that every eyeball is going to be trained on you and nobody will notice me stinking up the stage."

"You *are* doing great," Danny mumbled, more to himself than to anyone.

I looked around. Everybody was still staring at us—at me. The entire cafeteria saw me clearly, no hiding, no blending. I'd been outed in front of them all.

"Well, see you tonight, fair Kate, and don't say I didn't warn you, eh?" Josh said.

They loped away in that very certain way that guys like that move. Evan shot me a smile before he turned. I'd never been smiled at like that. My face burned. Travis, Lisa and I shamelessly joined everyone else in watching them saunter out of the Droopy Diaper. Then, when the guys were gone, the whole place seemed to turn back and look right at me. What now?

"That boy is such a moron," Lisa muttered.

"Which one?" Travis asked.

"All of them . . . well . . . the jury is still out on the new boy. I think I can see where Travis has a point, though."

"I do?" he asked.

"Yes, about our little Katie being smitten."

"I am not smitten!"

"She doth protest too much!" Travis said with a laugh.

Lisa clapped her hands. "Very impressive, quoting yet another Shakespeare play. *Hamlet*, I believe."

"I don't care if Hamlet came into the Droopy Diaper and said it himself, it isn't true!"

"You should at least look away from him when you protest," Lisa said.

I realized I was still staring in Evan's direction. I turned away.

"And close your mouth."

I closed my mouth.

"But for what it's worth, I do believe that Josh and Danny have also noticed *you*."

"Me?"

"My poor little Katie, you are such an innocent!" Lisa said.

"Sweet sixteen and never been kissed," Travis added.

My stomach seized but I kept my face blank. He was right—I had never been *kissed,* not really.

"You have to get used to people staring at you," Lisa whispered.

"I don't know if . . . I can't . . . I'm sure it won't . . ."

"Get used to it," she repeated.

She was right—being right was one of Lisa's uncanny abilities.

The effect had been just like being on stage. The new boy, Evan Campbell, had smiled at me, and presto, I was uninvisibled in front of the whole cafeteria. Just like that, he *saw* me, and then *they* saw me. It was official. Note the date and time. My world had changed . . . but how?

Chapter Eight

I looked back over my shoulder and she looked away, embarrassed. I could see her, but I couldn't tell what they were talking about. I turned away. There was no problem looking away from her. She was okay-looking, maybe cute even, but I didn't think I'd turn around to watch if she passed me in the hall. Each to his own, I guess. Or maybe my standards were just a little bit higher . . . no, there was no *maybe* there, my standards *were* higher. But still . . . there was *something*.

I looked back again. I caught her looking at me and she quickly turned away. Clearly I was the one *she* couldn't take her eyes off. Was she blushing? Katie Rosario was no femme fatale, that was for sure. I could tell that she was lacking in confidence, unsure of herself, and had no idea what she had going on. Then again, I thought it might make a refreshing change from the overconfident, arrogant princesses that I was used to dating.

A bell sounded—the five-minute warning. All around the cafeteria people got to their feet and gathered up their bags and trays and garbage.

"I'd better get to my next class," I said.

"What do you have?" Danny asked.

"Chemistry."

"You're in luck. That's my next class as well."

"Great. Fantastic." I got up and turned back towards where Katie and her friends had gotten to their feet. My eye lingered on her a little bit longer. I didn't see anything *that* special, but still, why was it that I couldn't stop looking?

Chapter Nine

The door to the back of the stage was open. I slipped in quietly and went into the room off to the side where I'd spent the last week working with the prop crew—that was part of my job. Along with Danny, we were building the scenes. Not exactly challenging, but I wasn't looking for a challenge, just marks good enough to graduate, get out of this school and get into university.

Danny was already there, along with Travis. They were talking about the set design. Travis was, to say the least, different. With all the black eye makeup, the white powder on his face and the black clothes, he looked like a photo-negative. And his conversations referenced everything from Aristotle to Disney movies—sometimes in the same sentence. He was smart, really smart. Smart people could be dangerous. The only people you could ever really truly trust were stupid people.

"Hey, Evan, how's it going?" Travis called out.

"Good, really good."

He came over and gave me a big hug. I gave him a sort of hug back. He seemed to do that with everybody, and the first time he hugged me I was so shocked I was speechless. While it didn't surprise me any more it was still a little disturbing. My family really wasn't exactly a hugging family.

"I was just telling Danny that I'm hoping the set will reflect the sensibility and subtle sensuality of the play," Travis said. "Not that I want to impinge on your own creativity, but it needs to have a certain panache."

"*Panache*?" Danny asked.

"Style, flair, flamboyance," I explained.

"Exactly, my darling! Exactly! Build with panache! Now I'd better go and talk to Ms. Cooper before I do a little directing."

Travis left.

"*He* has a certain flamboyance," I said to Danny.

"No question he has his own style."

"Yeah . . . I guess that's one word for it." I paused. "Do you think he's, um . . ."

"Gay?"

I nodded. Danny started to laugh. What did that mean?

"Is he or isn't he?" I asked.

"Just because he likes girls' makeup doesn't mean he doesn't like girls," Danny said.

"I just didn't know . . . don't tell him I asked that, okay?" I asked.

"It would just make him laugh," Danny said. "Although I think he jokes around because he isn't so sure himself."

"Really? Some guys would pop you just for suggesting they were gay."

"I don't think he could pop anybody," Danny said. "Are you afraid of him?"

"Afraid he might hug me too hard," I joked.

"Sounds a little homophobic to me. Hugs are nice."

"Then maybe he should hug *you* more often. It sounds like you might even enjoy that."

"Are you calling me gay, now?" Danny asked.

"Of course not! I was just—"

Danny started to laugh. Wow, I was going to need a playbill to sort these people out.

"Come on, we have to do a double-check of a measurement," Danny said.

Danny got up, grabbed the tape measure, and I trailed behind him.

Coming up to the stage from behind we could hear the actors rehearsing before we could see them. Standing at one side of the stage were Josh and Katie . . . well, really Petruchio and Katherina. We came in quietly from behind so we wouldn't disturb them.

Katie was good, better than good. She *was* the character. And Josh . . . well, he was Josh trying to play Petruchio in a foreign language— a language he apparently didn't speak or understand.

Danny grabbed a wooden sword and handed me a second. Playfully he poked at me and I defended myself. Ms. Cooper shot us a deadly stare, far more pointed than either of the wooden blades, and we put them down and started to work.

I held the tape measure and Danny measured while I listened and watched. I hadn't seen it at first but soon I got what they were saying about Katie. There *was* something different about her up there on the stage. The way she read the lines with such emotion, the look on her face, even the way her body changed. It was like she *was* Katherina— fiery and feisty and, well, somebody I might want to be with.

Chapter Ten

❦

Lisa wasn't kidding, she *had* memorized the whole play. Every single part, page and stage direction note. She could even keep the lines straight when we went out of order. Ms. Cooper levitated when she found out. Lisa was not even taking drama. Apparently, she'd started memorizing it the day I got the lead. Travis said she did it for me—for him, too, but mainly for me. He said she knew I was freaked. She wanted to help. No one had ever done anything like that for me. I sort of didn't know how to be with it. Travis said that's what friends did. No friend that I'd ever had before.

"*You* should've gone for the lead, you know?"

She smacked my head. "*I* know the words, *you* make them mean something. I've never seen anything like it, sweetpea. Just get out of your own way. Travis and me are here for you."

"Travis and I," I said.

She smacked me again.

So this was friendship. Thing is, Lisa and I didn't do sleepovers, each other's nails or never-ending phone calls. Neither of us knew how. She was curt, bordering on rude, even with Travis and me, and then she went and did this. So I did the only thing that made us both comfortable and ignored it, pretty much.

"Uh . . ." I examined Lisa from tip to toe on the way to rehearsal. "I, uh, love the thing you just did with your hair. Did you . . . shave that section? It looks . . . absolutely . . ." I so didn't want to offend her with the incorrect or poorly chosen adjective. "It looks absolutely . . . fierce!"

Lisa stopped and turned to face me and finally said, "You're welcome, Katie." The girl was a genius.

Josh and I took our places at the centre front of the stage. Other actors—including Pete Vukovic as Hortensio and David Gupta as Baptista—were at stage left practising their lines.

I noticed Evan and Danny come in quietly from backstage—everybody noticed. We all looked. Evan was hard not to look at. He was the opposite of invisible. They shuffled over to the stage prop corner and started goofing with the swords. Evan handled the weapon like he'd just walked off the set of *Spartacus*. Oh my. They put down the swords and started working with a tape measure.

I turned away from Evan, back to Josh. "How about if we start right here?" I said, pointing at his manuscript.

"Sure, that's as good as any place," he said.

I took in a deep breath and visualized Katherina. "*Mov'd! In good time! Let him that mov'd you hither. Remove you hence. I knew you at the first. You were a movable,*" I said.

Josh just shook his head. "What exactly is a movable?"

"A joint-stool," I answered.

"*Thou hast hit it . . .* um . . . *come, and,* um . . . *sit on me,*" Josh said.

"*Asses are made to bear, and so are you.*"

"Um . . . I'm sorry." Josh looked around helplessly. "It might help if I actually understood what her last line meant."

"She's saying you're a donkey," Evan called out.

We all turned to face him.

"An ass is a donkey. She said donkeys carry people and that makes you an ass."

"Nice language, Katie," Josh said. "No wonder you're a shrew. It would be so much easier if Shakespeare wrote this stuff in English."

"It is English," Evan said. "Just think about your next line . . . about how women are made to bear."

"You *know* my next line?" Josh asked in amazement.

"Not word for word. I just know what it means. You're just saying that she can have children."

"So I'm sort of propositioning her," Josh said.

"That's what you're doing throughout the whole first part of the play, you know, before you try to break her . . . tame her," Evan said.

"*That* I can understand," Josh said.

Danny and Josh exchanged smiles.

Travis and Ms. Cooper entered the auditorium.

"Let's get down to business!" Travis called out. "Let's take it from where we left it yesterday!"

I nodded and folded my script. I knew the next two bits, knew what they meant. It was always like that with Shakespeare, I just sort of "got" him. It seemed like Evan got him as well. Josh scrutinized his pages as if they held clues to a scavenger hunt.

"Okay, Petruchio, Katherina's a fireball, but remember, that's just because she's crying out for attention from her father."

Josh looked blank, not just confused, but nobody-is-home, power-failure blank.

I heard Lisa groan in the eighth row. I think Josh heard her as well.

"Okay." Travis started pacing. "Never mind that. You want her money, and you're such an arrogant jerk that you also want to show off your ability to bring Katherina down, make her *beg* for you."

"Okay!" Josh lit up. "The beg for it bit? I'm all over that!"

"Excellent!" Travis said, scanning his pages. "Katie, from line 214, please."

Oops. I drew a blank. I'd been too cocky in putting away my script. Now I would be punished. I deserved to be punished.

Lisa cleared her throat and I instinctively looked at her. She stuck her tongue out at me. That was all I needed. I remembered what that meant.

"*In his tongue.*" I winked at her.

"*Whose tongue?*" Josh asked, as if he wasn't even sure about the first line.

"*Yours, if you talk of tales, and so farewell!*" I turned to go. And then stopped, staring at Josh, waiting for him to deliver his next line. Even in the waiting, I could sense it, the power. All eyes were on me. Every fibre in my body lit up and waited for a response so that I could throw down another line and feel it all again.

"Oh, uh . . . hang on," he said. "Um . . . *what, with my tongue in your tail? Nay, come again. Now he takes her in his arms.*"

"Stop!" Travis yelled. Travis lifted his hands and slowly walked down the aisle and onto the stage until he was standing right beside Josh.

"Josh," he said, his voice so low that I could hardly hear him, "remember the italicized parts in your script are directions. So you take Katie in your arms there, you don't say, '*he takes her in his arms.*'"

Josh was squirming. I was squirming. I tried to give him a big booster smile, but I basically suck at that sort of thing. Danny and Evan moved to stage right, into my line of vision. My heart pounded a little louder.

"Okay, finish the speech, Josh," Travis said, encouraging him with a weak smile.

"Got it," Josh said. "*Good Kate, I am a gentleman—*"

I slapped him. "Ow!" He looked at me, genuinely shocked and hurt.

"Sorry, sorry!" I apologized instinctively.

"Petruchio, dear God, quit being such a pussy, she barely touched you. What are you guys going to do when it gets to real roughhousing?" asked Travis.

Josh's hand was still on his cheek. "No, I know, it was just a surprise, that's all." He looked at his script accusingly. "Oh, right, it's that italics thing again, isn't it? It says, 'She strikes him.' That's hit, right? It would help if I had clue one about what the hell they're talking about. Like, later on the page they're talking about cocks. Can we do that?"

"Chickens," I whispered so no one else would hear. "It's a rooster reference."

"So why's he talking about chickens?"

Travis looked like he was going to give birth. The rest of us didn't know where to look.

"I'm sorry, it just doesn't mean squat to me," Josh said.

Maybe he didn't understand the play but he did understand how bad he looked. I was embarrassed for him.

"I just wish I understood any of this . . . the way Katie does, and Travis, and Evan."

"Evan knows this play?" Ms. Cooper asked from her seat five rows back.

"Yeah, he was trying to explain some lines to me before you walked in," Josh said.

Ms. Cooper marched up the aisle, trailing pink and white chiffon scarves behind her. Evan looked like he'd been caught doing something naughty.

"Is that true? Do you know this play?" she asked.

"We took it at my last school, ma'am."

"Ma'am? Who says *ma'am?*" Ms. Cooper asked. "Katie, your next line."

"*No cock of mine, you crow too like a craven,*" I spat. Josh whistled and looked stunned at the same time.

"And, Evan, the line after that?" Ms. Cooper demanded.

Barely a second ticked by before Evan responded with a perfect, "*Nay, come, Kate, come, you must not look so sour.*" He locked on to me and did not look away.

It was the same line Josh had thrown out in the cafeteria—maybe he would have known that line, but still, Evan said it so, *so* much better.

My heart did that thing again. Was it Shakespeare or Evan? They both sort of had the same effect—a thrill that slowly boiled and bubbled up from the deepest part of me.

"Just as I thought," Ms. Cooper harrumphed. "Spoken like a young man who knows what the words mean and who, like our Lisa, has an eidetic memory. What are the odds?"

Josh turned to me, eyebrow raised.

"Photographic memory," I whispered.

"Evan, you have a new job," Ms. Cooper said.

"I like my present job."

"You'll like your new job even better," Ms. Cooper said. "From now on, you'll be explaining the text to our Petruchio here and . . ." She turned to Travis. It was like she suddenly remembered that he was there. "If that's all right with our director, of course."

"Works for me," Travis said. "Whatever makes the play lift off. So, Evan?"

"I can do that, ma'am," he said, while looking right at Travis.

Again with the *ma'am* thing. Somehow it was getting sexier every time *he* said it.

What was the matter with me? I was scaring myself. Who was I? I did *not* have these feelings, these thoughts. I actually tried to revive my horror movie obsession. Couldn't. Evan Campbell was right there standing next to Josh and, hence, next to me. All I could see was him and, boy oh boy, that boy was more distracting than *Carrie* and a symphony of construction noises.

Chapter Eleven

"Sounds like you've been sprung from working in the dungeon," Danny said. We were in the shop room working on the opening scene set.

"I'll still be offstage, so that's good." I paused. "And speaking of good, Katie is *really* good."

"And Josh really isn't. I feel sorry for—"

"Hey, guys!" Brittney called out as she poked her head into the room.

"Hi, Britt," Danny replied cheerfully.

I nodded an acknowledgement.

"Thank goodness it's Friday!" she said. Brittney was all lip gloss and legs—my usual menu pick.

"TGIF," Danny agreed.

"I'm thinking about a movie tonight. What about you two?"

"There are lots of good movies out," Danny said.

"I'm not much into movies," I replied. I turned to Danny. "How long does this set have to be?"

"Um . . . okay . . . see you later," Brittney sputtered, and then left.

"Man, did you shut her down."

I shrugged. "I just don't like most movies, especially the crap that comes out of Hollywood."

"I don't care that much for movies either, but there'd be nothing wrong with sharing some popcorn—or something else—with Brittney."

"I'm not into her type," I said.

"And her type would be beautiful and female . . . maybe it isn't Travis's sexual orientation that we should be questioning."

"Cute."

"And so just *why* aren't you interested in Brittney? She certainly is interested in you."

"She was talking to both of us," I said.

"She was looking at you."

"I didn't notice," I said. That was a lie. I could read the signs as well as he could. The problem was that she'd be too easy in the beginning and too hard in the end. "Besides, if she was interested in me it would have to do more with my car than my personality." I said that to make Danny feel better.

"It *is* a nice car."

"It's when she found out that I had the Audi that she seemed to take an interest in me," I suggested.

"I have an easy solution. Give me the car."

If only it were that simple.

"Better yet, you can keep the car and date *me*. At least I can admit that I certainly do *love* you for your car."

"Okay, so neither of you are my type. And before you ask, female is definitely my category. She just strikes me as being, I don't know, kind of high-maintenance."

"Well, I'd be prepared to put in a little maintenance work to keep *her* happy," Danny said.

"That's it, though, you probably *couldn't* keep her happy. My father once said to me that the best thing in the world is a beautiful woman."

"No argument there."

"But the *worst* thing in the world is a beautiful woman who *knows* she's beautiful."

Danny nodded his head knowingly. "And there's no question that Brittney knows it."

"Knows it and uses it," I said.

Danny nodded again.

"Keeping her happy would be a full-time job, and one you couldn't do successfully. Me, I'm just here for a few months and I'm not spending my time on somebody like her."

"I think I'd be prepared to *waste* my time on her," Danny joked.

"Then what's stopping you?" I asked.

"She didn't come here to flirt with me."

"She was flirting with my car," I said.

"Don't sell yourself short. If you were gay, and I were gay, you'd be up there pretty high on my list of guys I'd date."

"A fine compliment . . . although one that's making me increasingly uncomfortable," I joked.

I dug into my pocket and pulled out my keys and tossed them to him. He gave me a questioning look.

"You drive me home and then the car is yours for the night."

"You're joking, right?"

"No joke. Can you drive a standard?"

"I could. I know the principles behind driving standard."

"It's no big deal, it's a six-speed. I'll show you on the drive to my place."

"Won't your parents mind you lending out your car?" he asked.

"My father is still on another continent and my mother won't notice. Don't worry."

"It's not me who should be worried," he joked. "But I'll be careful, and I'll even fill up the tank."

"Don't waste your money. It's all on my father's charge card. Now, get out there and see if Brittney is interested in going to a movie tonight. Tell her that you and the Audi will pick her up."

Danny got up to leave and then stopped and turned around. He looked like he had concerns.

"Just go, be confident," I said. "Make sure you jingle the keys in front of her. Girls like her are fascinated by shiny objects."

Danny burst into laughter and left.

It was nice that the car was going to at least make him happy. I wished it could be that easy for me.

Chapter Twelve

Lisa and I walked away from the school and plopped down on a bench to wait for my bus.

"So you have a crush on Evan," she said.

"Evan? A crush? Well, maybe, maybe me and everyone else in the entire school. How about you?"

"Hmmm, so not my type." She turned to me. "Maybe it's even more than a bit of a crush?"

"Get real, Lisa, he doesn't even—"

"See you? Yeah, he does." She was getting scary-good at getting inside my head. She nodded, more to herself than anything. "I see who sees what. Always have." Lisa crossed her legs, right over left, and then uncrossed them. "Look, I was born, uh, *complex*. Thank God my units have the resources to deal with that. At least it makes them feel better." She crossed her legs again. This time left over right. "But you, I knew right off that you run deeper."

I stopped breathing.

"Keep breathing, Katie. Like I said, I see things. It helps me run circles around my shrinks."

"Shrinks, Lisa? Like, with an 's,' plural?"

She shrugged, but didn't say anything else.

And that was it. Note the date and time. That was the closest Lisa and I ever came to a normal girlfriend-to-girlfriend-type conversation. I was so stunned I would have let the first bus go by and at the very least talked about Evan some more, but Lisa was the one who reminded me.

"Hey, aren't you kind of late? I thought you said your old lady would massacre you if you let the play get in the way of your dinner-making and housekeeping duties."

Ooops, she was right. I was in trouble, big trouble. Mom was on day shift at The Flow, where she was a hostess. It's where and when she'd met her last three boyfriends. Mom hated days. The action was slow, so the tips were nonexistent, and she had to fill in the time by taking in stock and organizing supplies. It screwed up her manicures and her mood.

I flew out of the bus and out of the elevator, desperate to make it home before she did. It took a minute to register that there was noise in the kitchen. My stomach clenched.

"Mom?"

Pots and pans rattled. My mother barely knew where we stored them.

"Mom?" I called again.

"Naw, it's just me, kid."

Joey. He walked out with his tie flung over his shoulder and a tea towel tucked into his belt.

"Mr. Campana."

"I keep telling ya, call me Joey." He winked and I nodded. We both knew I wouldn't.

Joey Campana liked to think of himself as the silver fox. He had a monster head of shiny grey hair, I'd give him that—that and

a year-round tan that would make our school's orange crowd sick
with envy. He topped this off with an endless wardrobe of sharkskin
suits. Joey did not believe in "dress casual." Joey was a real estate agent,
a big one. Mom had hit pay dirt this time. The man had his face plastered on signs, bus shelters and concrete benches all over the city.

"I'm making my world-famous spaghetti carbonara."

"Right." I inhaled and smiled. "I smell that killer onion-bacon
combo."

That was a mistake. Joey stopped in his tracks, smiled back and
slid his eyes over me at the same time. Time froze, but I still had
enough juice left to will myself invisible. He whipped out the towel
and wiped his dry hands. Was he looking at me *that way*, the way
Mr. Kormos had? For the millionth time in the past few weeks,
I whipped back into a different time with a different one of my
mother's men. That was happening a lot lately. Why? Was it the
play? Punishment for being visible? It was messing me up something fierce. Memories, like rogue movie trailers, just kept shoving
themselves up and into my face.

Nick Kormos was boyfriend number two. Mom said she
loved him the best of all of them, including my dad. I was almost
twelve then and pretty stupid, stupider than now. I wasn't even
scared of "Call me Nick, kid." We lived with him in a massive
three-bedroom condominium. I didn't have the safety antennae
that girls are supposed to have. I actually *liked* Nick. Even when he
pinned me against the dining room table, I was more confused than
scared. Even with what had happened the times before, all those
little creepy things . . . I was shocked, immobile.

Like I said, stupid.

It was a miracle that Mom came home in time that day. She
wasn't supposed to get in until closing, four hours later.

I hated moving almost as much as she did. It was ugly.

She blamed me, but she didn't have to. I knew it was my fault. I was visible *and* stupid—a deadly combination.

Joey wasn't like that, though. I was pretty sure. And even if he was, I knew now how not to be there, how to stop it before it happened.

"Remember to keep at your mom that she needs a better stock of fresh ingredients, okay, kid?" He didn't pause for an answer. Instead, Joey returned to his bacon and onions. "So dinner's on me, eh? You can go relax and tweet your peeps."

Joey considered himself the master of all social media, and he probably was. Mom and I got non-stop lectures on how important Facebook, blogs and Twitter were to managing your standard successful real-estate empire.

I, on the other hand, considered myself the master of flying below the radar. I had and did none of those things. I was probably the only kid in the city without a cellphone.

Joey was crooning a Dean Martin song in the kitchen. He'd bought us an iPod and dock last Christmas and uploaded every Frank Sinatra and Dean Martin song ever recorded. Those two Italian dead guys seemed to have a million tunes. Anyway, Joey was safely singing "Volare" and muttering about the pathetic quality of our utensils. The point was that even when he was looking at me, he didn't see me.

I slipped into my room, shut the door and leaned against it. *Breathe in for three and out for four . . . breathe in for three . . .* Crisis averted. It was okay. I had done it. Apparently, I could turn it on and off. Good to know.

Chapter Thirteen

I heard the front door open and turned the TV up dramatically. I wasn't going to run out to greet her, but I wanted her to know where I was so she'd come to me.

She walked into the room in all her glory. It was the first sighting I'd had of her since last Sunday. She was wearing last season's Chanel and this season's Prada shoes, tasteful gold jewellery, and carrying her prized Hermes Birkin bag. The fact that I knew all that designer detail made me sad. Maybe Travis wasn't the only one with a hint of a sexual-identity crisis.

"That is incredibly loud!" my mother called out.

"What?"

"That is incredibly—"

I hit the mute button mid-sentence as she started to yell but stopped herself.

"I should really have your hearing checked," she said. "Too many years of wearing your iPod turned up too loud."

Too many years of needing to block out things I didn't want to hear.

"You would not believe what a week I had!" she said. "Every single charity seems to be running short this year. I'm on far too many boards."

I nodded my head. I wasn't going to argue about that. Didn't she know that charity began at home? "Would you like to know about my week?"

"Your week?"

"As in my first week at the new school . . . remember the new school?"

"Oh . . . I'm so sorry . . . you must think I'm a terrible mother!"

I didn't say anything. I just smirked.

"So, please, tell me, what was it like? I really want to know."

"I was expelled."

"You were expelled?"

I smirked again. "Just joking."

"That wasn't very funny. You shouldn't joke—"

"Actually, I got suspended."

"No! What did you do to get suspended?"

"Joking again. I wasn't suspended . . . but you have to admit that would have been better than being expelled."

She dropped her purse and slumped into a chair across from me. She looked tiny and bird-like. Rich covered up a lot of sins, but even expensive makeup, hair styled and coloured by "the best" and an occasional shot of Botox couldn't hide everything. My father and I had agreed to not mention her getting older. But we did notice, and not talking about it didn't change it.

"That was rather unkind of you, to kid me about being expelled," she said.

"Almost as unkind as you not remembering that I was forced to go to a new school in the first place."

"It's not as though we really had a choice."

"There are always choices. You decided *not* to pursue any choice that would have kept me in my school."

"Your father—"

"And we all know you wouldn't want to disagree with anything he said or did," I pointed out.

"Don't blame your father, Evan. It wasn't something that *he* did that started all of this."

I felt like I'd been punched in the stomach, and, judging by her expression, I could tell she knew and was feeling guilty. It was good she felt guilty for something, but really, how could I expect her to stand up to him on my account when she couldn't even do it for herself?

"I'm surprised you're home on a Friday night," she said, changing the subject.

"New school . . . remember . . . so no friends."

This she did deserve to feel guilty about, so I wasn't going to let her off the hook and tell her that I'd already made some friends.

"But I didn't see your car."

That she'd noticed. I couldn't very well tell her that I'd lent it to one of the new friends I didn't have.

"I brought it in for service. It was time for an oil change. You wanted me to be more responsible, right?"

"That *was* more responsible."

I actually impressed myself with how quickly I'd come up with a credible lie that not only covered up the situation but made me look good in the process. I guess there was more of my father in me than I liked to believe.

"It'll be back by tomorrow. They'll send the bill to you," I said.

"Not to me," she said, holding up her hands. "You know they should send it to our business manager."

"Okay, sure, I'll have them do that."

I bent down and pulled my calculus test out of my backpack and offered it to her. "Thought you might want to see this."

"What is it?" she asked as she took the paper from me. She looked concerned. Did she think it really was a suspension notice? She looked and—"This is a 98! That's a wonderful mark!"

"Not bad. Only two marks away from the mark that Dad would think is wonderful . . . or would he even be happy with that?"

"Don't be so hard on your father."

"Somebody should be hard on him." I got up from the seat and started to walk away before she grabbed my arm to stop me.

"He just wants what's best for you—for both of us. He's only hard on you to make you reach your potential."

"My potential would have been reached if you had fought to keep me in my last school rather than letting him sell me down the river. He could have worked things out and I could have stayed."

"Your father thought it was best, and obviously, judging by your calculus mark, his decision wasn't completely without merit."

I laughed. "Now if I do badly I'm wrong, and if I do well I'm wrong. There's no way to win with him . . . as usual."

"Don't say that."

"How the hell can you defend him after all that he's put *you* through?"

A shudder went through her whole body, as if I'd pierced her heart with an arrow. *I* hadn't. *He* had. But she still defended him. And, even after everything, she still stood by her man like some stupid country song. I didn't figure he'd stop test driving, I just wondered how long it would be before he got himself a new model.

"I just wish you didn't know," she said, her voice barely a whisper.

"If you could wish for anything, maybe it would be better to wish that it didn't happen at all."

"Not everything in life turns out the way you want. You learn to forgive and forget and move on, Evan."

"Maybe I'm not ready to forgive. And, believe me, I'm *never* going to forget," I told her. "But I am going to move on . . . as soon as I can."

Chapter Fourteen

I was trying to explain about Joey to Lisa and Travis while we were sitting on him, so to speak. We were on one of the benches he advertised on, the one in front of my bus stop. Joey's bench had somehow turned into our unofficial office, even though I was the only one of us who used that bus line. Come to think of it, I'd swear I was the only one in the whole school that got on that line. Travis had found me here back in September, recognized me from biology, sat down and gone into an impassioned rant on the colossal lameness of Weezer, which transformed seamlessly into his personal plan for world domination. My contribution was that I loved his smoky-blue eyeliner and told him so. We were best friends by the end of the week. Sounds easy, but Travis and then Lisa were friend experiments for me.

Maybe I was for them, too.

My mom and I moved every other minute, depending on which of her boyfriends we were living with. Too many neighbourhoods, too many schools—you can't get in tight with people when you live like that. No, that's not it. Friends, most of them anyway, want to know stuff, share stuff, compare secrets. Let's face it, that was the opposite of my modus operandi.

Except for me and Lisa and Travis. We let each other be with whatever we were carrying, and I'd bet my life that I wasn't the only one carrying a bit of dark.

Travis met us at the bus stop with three grande frappuccinos. It was a reward for yet another gruelling Josh/Petruchio rehearsal. The frappuccinos would have been my spending money for a week and tasted like they should be my calorie count for a month. What a brilliant, amazing thing, FRAPPUCCINO!

"So what's the deal with this Joey guy? Does he creep you out or what?" Lisa asked.

Travis turned around to get a better look at Joey's face. "Hmmm . . . I can never figure out whether I am repelled or attracted."

Lisa groaned. "You say that about half the girls in the school, too!"

"I am an all-loving love god and let's just leave it at that. But I'm not the important one here. I'm sensing an oddish vibe from our girl. Does Joey give you the willies, Katie?"

Since Travis had just forked out for my new very favourite thing in the world, I felt I owed him an answer.

"Joey?" I asked. "No. I mean, other than seeing and sitting on him all over the city, no."

We all leaned against Joey's photo, which pretty well covered the whole back bench, leaving just enough room for all of his business and social networking coordinates. I had an involuntary flashback to Nick Kormos. Again. Why was that happening so much? While Travis and Lisa slurped, I slipped back to that massive three-bedroom condo four years ago.

I was looking out of the floor-to-ceiling living room windows onto the tops of the trees, just standing and staring. Why? He came up behind me. Nick's reflection was crystal clear in the window. Was he smiling? I stopped breathing, then and now, and I didn't say anything, then or now. Nick's hands circled in front of me. I could see them in the reflection and when I looked down. He cupped his hands, and then pressed and pulled me back into him. His hands were on me. And I saw it all in the reflection in the window as if I were watching a movie rather than it being me. And then he groaned "Ahhh" and brought me back to reality.

Instead of gagging, I gulped down some frappuccino.

"No, not Joey," I said.

They both turned to face me.

"Well, I *know* I'm picking up a vibe," Travis insisted.

Right vibe, wrong guy.

"If he gets weird on you I'll . . ."

"What?" Lisa interrupted. "Spear him with your mascara wand, Emo-boy? When are you going to lay down and admit defeat, Travis? Emo is over, finished, kaput!"

It was a familiar and circular argument. Like Danny, Lisa didn't actually much care either way, but she loved razzing Travis about it.

"Hey!" he countered. "Anyone could have been Emo when Emo ruled—too easy. They were inauthentic Emos, if you will. Now that it's deader than a doornail, that, my dears, is when the true Emos come out. My melodrama is the real deal. It feeds my directorial genius!"

Lisa and I put our frappuccinos down and clapped. "Nicely done, Travis," I said.

"Okay," Lisa agreed. "We won't vote you off the Joey bench."

"I'm touched by your support." He slurped the dregs of his drink. "So, how are you feeling about the production in general and me as director in particular?"

Lisa groaned and answered before I could even think of an answer. "You're doing more than okay, and Katie's a showstopper, no crap. Who knew, eh?"

"See what happens when you decide to become visible?" Travis nudged me and I gulped. I kept forgetting that I told them stuff. Both of them. I'd spent so long floating around by myself that I forgot to keep a lid on stuff that should be lidded.

"And the new guy is gunning for her," Lisa said.

"Oh my God, Lisa! He *so* is not!"

"Evan checks you out from backstage and when he's giving Josh his lines. I am your prompter. I see and know all . . ."

"Well, I can see his appeal." Travis nodded. "And if he's smitten by our Katie rather than those plastic playthings like Brittney or Melody, etc., etc." Travis tossed his cup into the monster garbage can, which thankfully did not have Joey's face plastered on it. "Well then, there may actually be something to the guy," Travis said.

Lisa didn't say anything.

"Bus!" I yelled, happy to change the topic.

Lisa looked at her watch. "With time to make dinner and over half an hour to spare!"

They were way too familiar with my schedule. I was letting too much slip. Next thing you knew we'd be exchanging nail polish and secrets and . . . I would be without friends again. I dug out my pass from my jeans.

"Thanks guys, and thanks for the drink thingy, Travis. I've never had one before, it's my new favourite thing in the universe."

I jumped onto the bus and turned to wave before the doors closed. They both looked stunned. Probably shouldn't have said that about the drink. What self-respecting teen doesn't know the drink lineup from Starbucks?

I slumped down into the seat to give myself a good talking to and found myself thinking about Nick Kormos instead. I closed my eyes tight, trying to squeeze him out. I'd learned that you can't shut your head off, but sometimes you can cool it down a bit. The best way to do that was to substitute the problem image with a beautiful one. It muffled the bad noises and the icky feelings. I put in Evan Campbell for Nick Kormos. No problem. Those thoughts were nice and warm and, well, warm. I was getting very good.

Chapter Fifteen

"*Did ever Dian so become a grove as Kate this chamber with her princely gait?*" Josh said. He looked up at me. "Okay, Evan, so what the hell does that mean?"

"Dian refers to the goddess Diana." I lowered my voice, hoping that he'd follow my lead. We *were* in the library. "He's saying that Katherina, walking into the room—the chamber—is more beautiful than Diana walking through the woods—the grove."

"Okay, so that's like a big compliment."

"More like a fake compliment," I said. "It's not like he really believes what he's saying. He's just trying to manipulate her."

"Okay, that makes sense," Josh said. "Thanks."

"No problem." I paused. "I'm just not sure if helping you out like this is a promotion or a demotion from doing the set design."

"I'd consider it a real promotion if *I* could do set designs instead of the lead role. In fact, it might be a major promotion for the entire production if I was replaced."

"It is what it is," I said.

"I should have objected more in the beginning," Josh said.

"Would that have worked?"

He looked like he was thinking. "Probably not."

"I haven't really got Cooper figured out," I said.

"Welcome to the club."

Actually, she was kind of a sore point. What I did know was that Cooper didn't respond the way I expected her to. With most female teachers—most *females*—I could use a combination of politeness, charm and subtle flirtation to get around them. Strangely, Lisa gave off that same vibe—she didn't seem be falling for it. I didn't trust anybody else in the room who was smarter than me. I was glad that didn't happen very often.

"I don't mind admitting that I'm actually a little scared of Cooper," Josh said quietly.

"You're about twice her size. I think you just might be able to take her in a fistfight."

"It's not a fistfight I'm worried about—although I think she would put up a pretty good battle. That does sound stupid, doesn't it?" he asked.

I shook my head. "It's hard to feel comfortable when you haven't got a situation figured out."

"Well, never mind, it's one of the million reasons why I'm happy that you're helping. It's easier when I actually understand what the damn words mean," Josh said.

"Shakespeare's not really that hard."

"It is for me," Josh said.

"I guess it's only easier for me because I've been taking Shakespeare since I was in grade three or four. It's harder when you wait until high school to study this stuff."

"You were in private school, right?"

"I've been in *lots* of private schools."

"It must be hard to change schools," Josh said. "But that's probably why you've settled in here so well—lots of practice," he said. "I think I'd hate it."

"No, you'd do fine. You'd have a role to play: basketball star. I think Shakespeare had it right when he said, '*All the world is a stage and all the men and women merely players. They have their exits and entrances, and one man in his time plays many parts.'"*

"Is that from this play?" Josh asked.

I shook my head. "It's from *As You Like It*–a speech given by Jacques."

"I can't believe you know the words to different Shakespeare plays."

"Don't you know the words to songs you like?" I asked.

"I can recite almost every line from *Happy Gilmore*."

"*Happy Gilmore?*"

"You don't know *Happy Gilmore?*" He sounded not only shocked but almost disgusted.

"I don't know him," I admitted.

"It's not a him . . . well, it is I guess. It's simply one of the best movies ever made! Classic Adam Sandler, from 1996."

"'Classic' and 'Adam Sandler' are things you don't hear together very often," I said.

"He is a great actor. I don't know why he hasn't won an Oscar or two."

I had a pretty good idea.

"Anyway, he plays a hockey player who becomes a professional golfer. It's hilarious!"

"I'm sure it is. Like you said, this Happy guy had two roles that he played, hockey player and golfer, and that's probably why it was funny, because the two roles are so different."

"Very different and very funny," he agreed.

"So because you would have the role of basketball player you could fit in better," I said. "And now you have a very different role as an actor."

"Which I hope doesn't get me laughed at." He paused. "And what role are *you* playing?"

"I guess it depends on the person I'm talking to." That was way too honest, mainly because I hadn't expected him to come up with that question. Maybe he was more than just a jock. "But mainly I'm just being myself. And speaking of playing roles, there is your wife-to-be, Katherina."

Katie walked across the room and took a seat at one of the study carrels.

"She's quite the actress," I said. "How well do you know her?"

"Not really well. Outside of the play, Katie's really quiet. She might be different with her friends."

"Are any of those friends a boyfriend?"

"Aaahhh . . . I get it. To paraphrase Shakespeare, is boyfriend one of the roles you're hoping to play?"

"Maybe . . . why, you're not interested in her, are you?" I asked.

"Interested? That's putting it mildly. She is my betrothed . . . remember?" Josh joked.

"No, I mean, really, are you interested?"

"I've thought about it, but it would be way too confusing right now. You know, to be my girlfriend and my wife," he joked. "Especially since I have to spend so much time on basketball. And I do actually have a girlfriend already . . . nothing serious . . . but still time consuming."

"Sorry, didn't mean to disturb your marital bliss. But now that you've put it that way, I guess I can ask her out."

Josh looked a little thrown. "Okay, sure. But first things first—could we go back to my lines?"

Chapter Sixteen

A s I rounded the corner to our street, a car sped up, and
then stopped on a dime. An Audi. My heart cranked up its
volume. A silver Audi. There could only be one person behind that
darkly tinted glass. He hit his hazard lights, opened the door and got
out. *Thump, thump, thump.* Evan Campbell in all his glorious glory.

"Well, fancy meeting you here, Katie," Evan said as he leaned
against his car. It was hard to tell which was prettier. "Can I give
you a lift? It would be an honour." He gave a little bow.

I could barely hear myself think above my thumping heart.
Who was cranking up the volume? "No thanks, thank you. I'm, uh,
practically there."

The passenger-side window glided down. Someone else was
in the car. It was my supposedly beloved, Josh.

"Hey, Katie!" He stuck his head out the window. "Great
rehearsal. Again. Could you be just a little less, you know, good? I'd
really appreciate it."

"He's kidding." Evan smiled. "He knows that no one will notice
Petruchio, Petruchio won't even exist as long as you're on stage."

"Great, if *that* doesn't make me feel better I don't know what
will," Josh muttered back.

"Well . . ." Evan smiled right at me. Strange, that smile. How
did he do that? "You are *that* good." *Thumpa, thumpa . . .* His eyes

were actually green, not blue as I'd originally thought. And his hair was a bit darker than your standard Palm Beach blond. I'd never had an excuse to stare right at him for this long. So I did. Evan had really dark eyelashes and eyebrows, which was unusual for golden girls and boys. And he was tall, almost as tall as Josh. I'd got that part right.

"So, Katie, I'm not much of a movie guy, but there's this really good documentary playing."

Why was he telling me this? Had I missed something?

"Yeah, so, the word is that it's a killer documentary about this ghetto school in Mumbai. What do you say? Friday night? It's playing at the Carlton."

What did I say about what? Friday night? What Friday night? What movie? Dear sweet holy . . . "Wait, wait! Are you asking me out? Like, on a date? You and me?" Oh God, I'd said that part out loud, and with all the practised aplomb of a girl who has never in her entire life been on a date.

Big luscious smile. "Uh huh," he nodded.

Words, I had to pay attention to the words. Pull yourself together, Katie, you're an actress! You are a good actress! Brilliant, I was referring to myself in the third person. *Oh, that way madness lies.* Quoting *King Lear*? It was official, I was certifiable.

"Since you are my betrothed, he sought out my approval, my dear Katherina," Josh said.

I bent down to face Josh. What was he blathering on about, and why was he always better off the stage than on it?

"And I gave him my permission, grudgingly," he added.

I turned back to Evan. "So you're asking *me* out, really?"

"That would be the idea," he said. Again with that killer smile. Evan Campbell was a walking Colgate ad.

"Yeah, sure, okay, great. So, uh, seven? Wait, you didn't say the time. I shouldn't say the time. You should say the time. What time?" I stuttered.

What was I doing? Was this really happening? Evan smiled again. At me. That boy was definitely smiling *at me*. That fact alone made being visible worth it, and worth anything that might come from the fallout.

"Seven is good," he agreed. "Where do you live?" He glanced uncomfortably at the mangy crop of high-rises that made up my block.

"No, don't bother! I'll be downtown anyway," I lied. "How about we meet at the theatre?"

"Whatever suits you best." He stepped towards me to . . . to what? We never found out, because Josh tooted the horn. I jumped back fifty feet.

"Hey, guys, I'm all for young love, but could this happen a little faster?" Josh yelled out.

Evan winked at me. "See you at rehearsal tomorrow."

"No!" Okay, that came out way too loud. I startled both of us. "No rehearsal tomorrow, remember, and just a script review on Friday, so I'll see you at the theatre, the *movie* theatre, I mean."

Evan looked a bit uncertain. "You'd better give me your cell number."

"Don't have one." That shut him down. I could see him struggle not to look surprised. "But don't worry, I'll be there for sure, absolutely. And if you aren't, I'll still go in. Like you said, it sounds like a great story. Bye." I turned and walked away before I could say another mind-numbing, idiot, brain-rot, stupid thing.

I heard the car door shut. He gunned the Audi and I watched it recede into the distance.

Okay, sit-com dialogue aside, did Evan Campbell just ask me out? Was I being punk'd? Were we back to the Stephen King thing? Was I having a heart attack?

See me?

There would be no avoiding me. I was putting out ear-splitting heart thumps that could be heard from a block away. It was a toss-up which was going to make me more visible, starring in the school play or going out on a date with Evan Campbell. My money was on Evan, that's how big his star power was.

I tore off for home. There were only two days to prepare. There was so, so much to do. I knew that. Now, if only I'd had a clue as to what, exactly.

Chapter Seventeen

O h. My. God! Too much, too fast, too good! At least for me. We, I, maybe we, had a great time. If I never had a date again in my entire life—and I figured I probably wouldn't—at least I'd had a brilliant first and last date!

Lisa and Travis had gone into overdrive on the prep, although, come to think of it, I don't remember either of them boasting about their dating histories before this. Pinned against a wall, Lisa just kept saying that she'd had a whole rich tapestry of experiences before she'd met the two of us. I, for one, believed her. Not to be outdone, Travis hinted darkly about dark love in dark places. None of us much bought into that, including Travis, I think.

I kept reminding myself that I'd been watching my mom prep my whole life. But then again, that was for old guys, different ball game. Besides, I didn't own anything that skanky.

Lisa lent me a cobalt-blue cashmere sweater to go with a fifteen-dollar pair of black skinny jeans that I bought on sale at Old Navy. Travis mascaraed and lip-glossed me endlessly until he was finally satisfied with the combination of dark and shiny. And for two days we rehearsed first-date small talk and witty repartee.

By the time I hit the subway, my anxiety about what I looked like had been replaced by my anxiety about whether Evan would even show up or not. Was this all just a big goof, a prank, like the *Carrie* movie? Had I imagined the whole thing?

To make matters worse, I was twelve minutes early. That was an extra seven hundred and twenty seconds to panic. But he was there! Unbelievably, Evan Campbell was already there, waiting for me right by the movie poster. I was laughably grateful to him and we hadn't even said hello.

"Hi." He smiled. "I wanted to make sure you didn't have to wait. You look terrific, Katie."

Evan fanned the tickets in front of me to show he'd already got them. "I really hope your parents don't mind that I didn't come over to meet them."

Wow, what century was he from? I knew less than nothing about dating, but even I knew that no one came over to get checked out by dear old dad these days.

"No," I said. "It's just my mom, and she's already gone to the cabin with her boyfriend."

It was true. Mom, who always said that fresh air made her puke, had somehow convinced Joey that she shared his obsession with rocks, scrub maples and the great outdoors.

"Oh, I'm sorry. Did I mess up a great weekend away for you?"

"No." And I left it at that. They'd been going almost all spring, summer and now autumn, whenever Joey could get a weekend away. I'd never been invited. Mom told Joey that I was allergic to leaf mould or something to explain why I *couldn't* come along. What she told me was, "Not a chance! There's no way I'm going to have your whiny butt getting in the way of a good thing. Not this time, sugar plum!"

Whiny? I was whiny? I wasn't whiny. I didn't mean to be whiny. Then I noticed Evan taking me in.

"You look really pretty in that shade of blue, Katie. I don't think I've seen you in it before. Cobalt, you should wear it all the time."

"Thank you, Evan, you look very handsome as well."

Aaaaarrrgh! *Very handsome as well?* Travis and Lisa had been coaching date conversation for two full days, and I came up with *very handsome as well?*

He smirked. No, not a smirk, it was a chuckle, definitely an indulgent chuckle. "So, movie first, then how about a bite at Mexicali Rosa's?"

I must have nodded. Movie *and* dinner, dear God. What should I pay for? What was I *supposed* to pay for? And did I have enough money to pay for it? Lisa had said that since Evan did the asking, the first date was generally on the guy. *Generally.* But this was two things, a two-parter, so now what? I wasn't even hungry. We'd had pizza at Lisa's pre–lip gloss, an hour ago. My mind went in propeller mode, circling and circling. The movie wouldn't be over until after nine. Who ate after nine? How expensive was Mexican food? Mexican didn't sound expensive. Maybe I could just have tacos and a Coke. I could afford that if he didn't go to town on some big Mexican number. Was Mexican food expensive?

I'm sure the movie was brilliant, and I certainly told him it was, but I could have been at a car wash for all that I was paying attention. Instead of focusing on the film, I worried about whether I was sitting correctly, whether my lip gloss was still on, would he kiss me, and what happens to lip gloss when you kiss? And more than anything, I worried about not having enough money for the dinner part.

Everything changed the minute we walked into the restaurant. It seemed like every single person in the place knew Evan!

The guy that sits you down, the waiters and even the cook or the chef or whatever you call him came out to shake his hand. That calmed me down. Surely, the girl wouldn't be expected to pay in a place where they all hovered around the guy. I relaxed for the first time since I'd got on the subway.

Evan ordered for me and then showed me how to layer and properly fold a sizzling fajita. I felt so sophisticated. The fajita was delicious and perfect and I ate it all, plus the fried banana thingies for dessert. I had never tasted anything that good, ever. And rather than making me feel stupid about not having done this kind of thing before, dating and dining I mean, Evan really seemed to enjoy showing me.

And it wasn't just about fajitas. Evan seemed to know everything about everything. He had lived around the world and done things that I could never even have dreamed about doing. Evan knew how to eat an artichoke and what to do if an avalanche is coming. He also knew where the best bargains were in the Lower East Side in New York, and how to play cricket, or was that croquet? I always get the two mixed up. He wasn't being all show-offy about any of it or rubbing it in my face. We were just talking. And you'd have thought a guy like him would just want to talk about himself, but no! Here he was so amazing and all, and he wanted to know about me.

"So your father is . . ."

"Gone." I shrugged. "He took off before I was three. I don't know where he is now. My mom says he hated being a dad." Okay, could that have sounded more pathetic? I'd have to make up something stupendously cheerful if he asked me any more about my home life. Instead we talked a bit about his other schools, and then he wanted to know about my friends. Thank God I had some to talk about.

"So Travis, our ever so talented director and all-round good Goth guy?"

"Emo," I corrected. "I guess they didn't allow either at your other schools." And we were off, just like that, chatting, smiling and laughing like any other normal couple on a date. I'd even started breathing by the time coffee was served.

"Your mom never remarried?"

Not for lack of trying, I thought. "No, she's really, really gorgeous, but, you know, she's got baggage—me."

I tried smiling to minimize the damage as soon as I realized what had just slid out of my mouth. Evan seemed to be examining me, weighing something, then he reached across the table and put his hand over mine.

"Don't do that."

What? Was he angry?

"Don't *ever* say or think that about yourself. You are a star, Katie Rosario, in every single way." I think I shook my head because he continued. "You have got to see you the way I see you. You're amazing."

He made me feel all floaty and fine.

"And the whole school will see just how good you are on opening night. Years from now I'll be telling *People* magazine that I was the one who showed you how to layer a fajita."

I almost believed him. Enough so that I had a medium-sized panic about my clothes. I was going to need a better wardrobe if I was going to be this star and be *seen* all over the place.

"Do you like my jeans?" I asked, apropos of absolutely nothing.

Evan looked a bit embarrassed. "Uh, Gap?" he asked.

"Old Navy," I admitted. "The sales bin."

I could tell by his expression that he didn't know what I was talking about. His pink-and-blue-striped shirt probably cost more than my entire wardrobe.

"I'm thinking that, uh, maybe the cashmere sweater suits you better," he said. "You strike me as somebody who should be in cashmere, all the time."

I almost blurted out that the first time I'd ever even felt cashmere was when I'd slipped on this sweater, but I stopped. "This old thing? I'm so glad you like it!" I tried to match his smile. Maybe I could get Lisa to never wear the sweater again. This guy noticed stuff. What other guy would know cobalt blue?

"Thing is, thanks to the play, I've had to claw my work hours back at the bakery to practically nothing, which has had a disastrous impact on my current wardrobe," I said, desperately trying to provide an excuse for my shlumpy clothes.

"You've got the lead in the school play *and* you work?"

"Well, like I said, not as much as I used to." I glanced at my watch. "Crap, it's almost midnight! How did that happen? Sorry, I'm so sorry, I have to go now. If you don't mind, that is."

Evan looked puzzled.

"I loved every single minute and second, but I've got a double shift at the bakery tomorrow, starting at 4:30."

Now he looked stunned. "4:30? Like, a.m.? A double shift? Man!" He shook his head. "Well, I was hoping we could get together tomorrow night, but you'll just be getting off shift. Next Friday, then?"

Wait, wait. What had just happened? Had he just asked me out *again*?

"I'm sorry . . . what did you say?"

"Do you want to go out with me next week?" he asked, throwing a million-volt smile at me.

I burst out laughing.

"That's not the usual reaction I get. Is that a yes or a terrible rejection?"

"A yes!" I practically screamed. Calm down, calm down, calm . . . "God, yes!"

"Good. But do you have the same schedule next week?"

I nodded.

"Then Friday night it is."

"Great, okay, super!" I jumped up, ready to dart for the subway. "See you at rehearsal on Monday!"

Evan jumped up too and grabbed my wrist. "No, Katie. Please, I insist. It's late, I must drive you home. It wouldn't be right to let you go home at night alone and unprotected."

"Oh, oh right." I looked at my wrist—him holding my wrist. It felt so warm and strong and tender, all at once. "Sure, fine. That'd be great, but . . ."

"I won't come up," he promised. "I'll just see you to the doorman."

My stomach pitched. My real life kept getting in the way. "No, it's not like that. No doorman, Evan, it's not, our apartment is . . ." He'd find out, everyone knew what those apartments were. "It's, we got a, it's city housing."

Mom had pinned all her hopes on Joey and all her money on "Mommy maintenance," as she called it. Her clothes, her hair, her spa stuff. She was the *investment*.

"We'll be moving soon, though."

"To the lobby, then!" Big smile.

As useless as I was about this stuff, I could tell that Evan was going out of his way to make it easy for me. And for some stupid reason, I was close to tears as a result.

As usual, the streetlights were out in front of our building.

Evan put the car in park, leapt out and around and opened the door for me. I could feel my blood pumping even before he took me in his arms. The crispness of his shirt, the trace of aftershave that made him smell like a walk on the beach.

Not that I ever have.

And he was so strong.

Maybe Evan didn't play basketball like Josh, but when he held me I knew that he could take on Josh and win. He was even stronger than Nick Kormos. My eyes readjusted and I took him in. God, he was lovely. Evan tightened his grip even more. I gasped, but I don't know why, I'd never felt safer.

"Good night, Katie," Evan whispered, and then he lifted my chin with the crook of his finger. Small, sweet, sweet smile. "Thank you for a wonderful evening."

And then he kissed me on the mouth so gently that I almost fell apart.

Chapter Eighteen

We walked hand in hand. It was harder to move through the crowded halls, but she liked it when we walked that way. I could tell she liked being seen with me. I liked it too, but maybe for a different reason. It was like marking my territory. *This* belonged to me. This was *mine—my* girlfriend. Then again, maybe her reasons weren't so different after all. I knew she liked people—okay, not people, other girls—to know that I was her boyfriend of three weeks.

Up ahead was a group of girls—*the* group of girls. They were the ones everybody looked to for direction, the ones who controlled fashion, who decided what was in and what was out and, more important, *who* was in and who was out. Whether they were strutting the hall like it was a fashion runway, holding court at their table in the cafeteria or strategically posing outside the main doors, they knew they were the nerve centre of the school. All the girls wanted to be them and all the boys wanted to be with them—except for one, me.

It hadn't taken me more than a couple of days to figure out who they were. It had taken me even less time to decide that they weren't the group I was going to hang with. Not at this school. Not this time. I could have if I'd wanted to. I *still* could. They were mine for the taking, but I didn't want any. Funny, but somehow not wanting any of them made them want me even more. They were used to having guys stumble all over them, so I was a source of confusion, frustration and attraction. Human nature—if they wanted me before, now that they couldn't have me they wanted me even more.

There was a fine line I had to walk when I was around them—I couldn't ignore them completely or they'd know I was deliberately doing it and thus was really noticing them, but I couldn't give them too much attention, either. I gave a subtle nod of my head in their direction and most of them flashed me a big smile, which I promptly ignored.

Katie, of course, wasn't part of their group. She didn't have the clothes or the money or the attitude. She wouldn't have been able to play the games they played—hell, I didn't even think she knew there was a game going on. Another one of the reasons I liked her.

"Hey, Evan," Brittney sang out as we passed by.

I gave her a disinterested wave.

"Hello . . . Katie."

"Hi, Brittney," Katie replied. "How are you?"

Brittney ignored her, of course. Katie hadn't picked up either the flirtation in Brittney's voice or the subtle digs—the hesitation before saying her name, like she didn't know it, or like Katie was so insignificant that you couldn't expect somebody as *important* as Brittney to remember her or answer a question.

I knew that they wondered why I was dating Katie instead of one of them. Although at this point I thought Katie probably could have become at least an honorary member in their little group—at least if she dropped Lisa and Travis. They were so far down the social evolutionary scale that they could never be much more than what they were. I'd elevated Katie's status . . . or, as my father would say, I had increased her *market value*. I *hated* when I even *thought* like him.

I actually wondered if other people were beginning to see in Katie what I saw. I was giving her confidence, and that confidence was sexy, like an aphrodisiac. She smiled more these days. She was more comfortable in her skin . . . her beautiful, perfect skin.

We kept walking. I didn't need to look back to know they were watching us—thinking, wondering, trying to make sense of us as a couple. Maybe they didn't know why I was with her instead of them, but *I* certainly did.

Dating one of those girls would have involved way too much energy and time—listening to their boring stories about the stupid things that interested them, hearing about their lives and their friends, trying to prop up and feed their egos, having to spend time doing things I didn't want to do, taking phone calls I didn't want to take, and, in the end, no matter how hard I tried, it still wouldn't have filled the gap in their vapid souls. They weren't looking for a boy-friend, they wanted a mirror to reflect back their own image.

Katie, on the other hand, didn't make demands. She was just happy that we were together, period. She was thrilled when I asked her anything about what she was doing, and she was so impressed with whatever I had to say about anything. I knew that she had never looked at anyone the way she looked at me.

I spotted Travis and Lisa up ahead but they didn't see us before they turned down the hall, and I made sure that Katie didn't see them by pulling her into me for a "spontaneous" kiss. It was a brilliant move on my part, if I do say so myself. On the one hand, it was in full view of the cool girls and raised Katie's coinage even further, and on the other hand, we avoided bumping into Creepy and Creepier.

Okay, I had to admit that I was sort of getting used to Travis—he was a pretty good director, and he did know how to put on makeup better than most of the girls in the school—but he still unnerved me a bit. Lisa, on the other hand, was somebody I could just do without completely. She didn't seem to be buying what I was selling. I was starting to think that maybe she wasn't interested in my "product." Maybe she was buying from the other side of the counter. Maybe the reason she didn't like me was because she saw me as competition for Katie. I'd keep my eye on that action. Not that I was worried. Katie was mine against *all* comers, no matter which side of the plate they batted from. I just thought it was best to stay away from Lisa, and keep Katie away from her as much as possible as well. Katie was so much better than that, better than them. Slowly I was weaning her away from them. She wasn't complaining. Lunches with me on the lawn were so much more enticing then joining them in the cafeteria.

Katie blushed and then flushed hotter than a gas fire as soon as I let her go. I do that to girls. Quick little check to make sure that the Brittney Posse had caught that—yup, mouths still open. I squeezed her. Katie gasped and then gave me a shy little smile. I started to come to the uncomfortable realization that my newest girl might be a virgin. Okay, potentially problematic, but maybe even better in the grand scheme of things.

I led Katie away, still holding onto her hand. We went to the far corner of the cafeteria. There were a number of empty tables. I settled in, taking a seat with my back practically against where the two walls met. If I had a choice I always sat with my back against the wall. Not only did it give you a view of everything that was happening, it also made sure that nobody would come up on you from behind. I knew I wasn't Wild Bill Hickok, and I wasn't playing poker, but still . . .

"Where do you want to start?" Katie asked.

"How about right here." I opened up her book and flipped to Act IV, scene 3.

She nodded her head. I knew she didn't like that monologue but she'd have to get to it sooner or later.

"You and Grumio enter and he says, *No, no, forsooth, I dare not for my life!*" I said.

"*The more my wrong, the more his spite appears. What, did he marry me to famish me? Beggars that come unto my father's door upon entreaty have a present alms. If not, elsewhere they meet with charity. But I, who never knew how to entreat...*"

It happened again, she transformed in front of me. She was no longer just Katie, but Katherina, the shrew in need of being tamed. She was wild and strong-willed, beautiful and alluring. And mine. And more and more I was seeing that same quality even when she wasn't on stage.

"*Am starv'd for meat, giddy for lack of sleep, with oaths kept walking, and with brawling fed...*" She paused.

"*And that which spites me,*" I said, prompting the next line.

"I know the line," she said, suddenly becoming Katie again. "It's just I was thinking about what this is all about. Petruchio won't let her eat or sleep."

"That's how he's breaking her," I said. "Taming the shrew."

"But in world politics class we were hearing about the way that political prisoners are broken down using techniques like starvation and sleep deprivation. It's more like she's his prisoner than his wife."

"In those days the two weren't that different," I said. "A woman belonged to the husband, and before that the father. She was simply chattel."

"Sorry? I don't..." She looked down at the table.

"It's not your fault." I reached over to touch her cheek. "Blame the public education system. Chattel means property, really anything owned by the man, like his cows or wagons or wife. Wife, kids, lock, stock and barrel! Women and children weren't people, they were human property, basically his slaves."

"That's awful!"

"That's why they call them the good old days, I guess."

"That's even more awful!" she said while punching me in the arm.

"You know I'm just kidding around." Sort of. It sure would have been easier back then—for the man. Divorce didn't mean losing half of all you'd worked for; it was simply turning in one model for another. I was pretty sure that was what was keeping my father around—fear of losing half of everything that he loved . . . and that wasn't me or my mother.

"I just can't get over you," Katie said. "I used to think I was pretty smart until I met you."

I gave her my best indulgent smile.

"Sometimes I feel a bit stupid compared to you."

"Just compared to me?" I questioned.

She looked shocked, but then she said, "Well, you and Lisa. She's scary-smart too."

I clenched my teeth. Clearly it was too early to separate her completely.

"But really, there's nobody like you, nobody knows the things you do!" she said.

I reached over and took her hand. "Thanks, but there's lots of things I don't know. For example, why Cooper picked *Taming of the Shrew* as the play."

"What do you mean?"

"Think about it. She's a raving feminist who's always talking about equality and women's rights and she picks a play in which Shakespeare presents women as possessions of their fathers and husbands. That doesn't make sense."

"Maybe that's why she did it," Katie said, "to show us how far we've come and to show us women not to take our freedom and rights for granted."

I shrugged. "Maybe, it's just that I can't figure her out."

"What's to figure out? She's a great teacher."

"No, she's a *good* teacher. I just can't figure out why she doesn't like me."

"What? She likes you! Of course she likes you!"

"I think she likes me about as much as Lisa likes me," I said.

"That's crazy talk. Lisa adores you!" She was shocked, but also a bit uncertain. It had worked. "And Ms. Cooper likes you too. In fact, everybody likes you! I've never seen anything like it. You've been here a minute and the whole school loves you, so of course Lisa and Ms. Cooper do too. How can you even think that they don't?"

I almost blurted out my reasons: at least one of them had me figured out, and one was maybe jealous. "Nothing I can put my finger on . . . just a feeling," I said.

"Well, I just know that her putting me in the lead role means so much to me. I don't know why she did that."

"Who else would she put in that role? You are a *spectacular* Kate."

She started to blush. I didn't know girls still actually did that.

"You're just saying that because . . ." I could tell she was going to say one thing and then she switched up to another. "Because you're so sweet."

"I'm saying it because everybody is saying it, because it's true."

She gripped my copy of *The Taming of the Shrew* with both hands.

"I never lie," I said—which of course was a lie. "And I'll never lie to *you*." Which was an even bigger lie. She melted before my eyes.

"I'm going to tell you something that I've never told anybody."

I had this sinking feeling that she was going to tell me that she loved me, and then I'd have to either lie to her and tell her that I felt the same thing or—

"I want to be an actor," she said.

"Really?"

"You don't think I'm good enough to be one?" She sounded devastated.

"No, I don't think that at all. You are an incredible actress!" At least that wasn't a lie.

She blushed again. It was kind of a rush being able to do that.

"It's just that before being in this play I would never have thought anything like that," she said. "I was always too nervous to even answer questions in class . . . but now . . . up there on stage . . . it, I feel *so* right."

"It *is* right. I don't think you *could* be an actress. You *are* an actress."

She leaned in close. "If I tell you something else, will you promise not to tell anybody?" Her voice was just above a whisper.

"You know you can count on me." The lies were adding up.

"Ms. Cooper has arranged for some people from the National Academy to come to the opening night performance. She thinks they might offer me a summer internship with a real possibility of a scholarship after graduation next year."

"That's wonderful!" I kissed her hair.

"Please, Evan, don't, not here," she whispered.

I bit back a rush of anger—who was she to tell me what to do?—but I held it inside. "I'm sure once they see you they'll offer you a full ride."

"Oh, Evan, it means so much that you believe in me."

And right at that moment, even *I* wanted to believe I wasn't lying.

Chapter Nineteen

Evan and Katie, Katie and Evan, Evan, Evan, Evan! It was a prayer when I was happy, and a mantra when I was scared, like every single time we walked down the halls together. I think it was that whole *Carrie*/pig's blood thing again. Something bad was bound to happen. It always did—both in those horror movies and in my life. But then again, it was a major miracle we were together to begin with. It had been twenty-six, no, twenty-seven days so far, so why shouldn't it last?

I think Lisa had already made a decision that not only *wouldn't* it last, it *shouldn't* last. I couldn't figure that out. Lisa had started out so supportive—well, for Lisa, that is. She'd loaned me a ton of stuff and tried to get me up to speed on the dating rules. But more and more, Lisa had less and less of anything to say about Evan. It wasn't that she said anything bad about him, she just didn't say anything at all. She'd change the topic whenever I said his name, which also was less and less, because I didn't have much free time to see her or Travis, outside of school or rehearsals.

Evan knew she didn't like him. I kept telling him he was way wrong, but he knew. He knew before I knew. He was *so* smart.

Evan was, hands down, the *best* thing that had ever happened to me in my whole life, ever. You'd think my so-called best friend would have been over the moon for me. Instead she moaned about me never being anywhere I should have been—which meant being with her.

But what could I do? I had Evan.

I had to admit that I loved to see the looks on the faces of the school *royalty* when we walked by. Lisa said that every school in the universe has them. Girls with more money than brains. Most of that money went into clothes, weekly blow-outs and regular visits to the Tanning Salon, hence the *Orange crowd*. They used to make me glad I was invisible.

But they didn't have Evan. I did. And *my* Evan just kept coming up with unbelievable little surprises for me. Like last Friday. First we met for gourmet hamburgers, and who else would have known there even was such a thing? And then, for the surprise, we drove to a movie revue house for a single-night showing of Elizabeth Taylor and Richard Burton in 1967's *The Taming of the Shrew*! Apparently, Evan had scoured the city for something that would be special for me! I couldn't even speak afterwards.

How could I not love him? And I did. Let's face it, I'd been gone on Evan Campbell from the minute he'd walked into drama class almost a month ago, and that was before he'd become my Prince Charming and my Knight in Shining Armour all rolled into one. The way he smiled just for me, touched my hand and explained things to me. I felt so safe when I was with him, protected, like nothing and no one could hurt me. I loved him, but I couldn't think it, write it or say it. Especially not to him. My mother—and God knows, she had more experience than most—had told me, at least a million times, that the best way to drive a man away was to talk about commitment or feelings. "Open your mouth and jinx the whole thing."

She should know.

Still, the words were desperate to erupt and free themselves. He did so many adorable things. Like on Tuesday, we were walking down the hall together, towards Ms. Cooper's class. There they were right outside the biology lab, the best of this year's *Orange* crop. Brittney, Tiffany, Jessie and Melody. I saw Brittney elbow Melody, who then promptly bounced over to Evan, leading with her chest. She used her breasts like they were weapons.

"Hey, Evan, what's up?" Melody threw back her shoulders and flashed her best bleached pearlies at him. They just weren't going to give up. Evan thinks I don't notice. They barely acknowledge me. I notice. Just because I was invisible all those years doesn't mean I didn't *see* everything. And that day they *saw* me, all right. How could they not with Evan holding my hand? Besides, I happened to be wearing a fabulous peach Juicy Couture outfit. Lisa had hauled it out of the back of her little sister's closet for me. Even though it was almost practically new, it was either for me or the Goodwill, she said. I'd never owned anything so designer classy in my life. There was no way Melody didn't see, no matter how hard she was concentrating on disappearing me. Hey, the only person who was allowed to make me invisible was me.

I see it all in slow motion. Melody bats her breasts at Evan and says, "There's a little 'do' at Brittney's on Friday. We would *love* it if you came, Evan."

Then nothing. It's like he's gathering himself. Evan puts his arm around me really tight. It almost hurts. He's just so incredibly powerful. Evan has no idea how strong he is. "Sorry, Melody," he says, "but my girl and I already have plans for Friday night. I'm taking her home for dinner."

Melody didn't know whether to spit or swoon. I hit pause and replay on the *"my girl"* part and kept hitting it until she huffed away. We walked by them with Evan's arm still around me.

When we got just past Brittney, he leaned over and whispered in my ear, "Are you okay with that, Katie? I should have asked you first, of course. If you'd rather go to the party . . ."

"I don't think it was me that they were inviting," I said.

"Hey." He brushed a strand of hair off of my face. "Even those airheads wouldn't be stupid enough to think that I'd go anywhere without you. So, is it okay that we skip it? I do want you to come over to my house."

I just nodded. A word would have not been possible, a full sentence was completely out of the question. Evan kissed my hair. They were looking, of course. I could feel the heat of their eyes on my back. He'd done all that for me. That whole thing had been a performance for the *Oranges*. Never mind Petruchio, even Romeo could have taken lessons from Evan. *My Evan.*

Putting the *Oranges* in their place was like scaling a mountain just for me. I got carried away and told him so when we met for frappuccinos after rehearsal. It wasn't like telling him that I loved him or anything, so that was okay. Right?

". . . and I'm so, so glad that I wore my new outfit. You always say how image is important."

He got busy examining the dregs of his drink.

"It's brand new. Well, for me. You haven't said anything. Do you like it?"

"The thing is, Katie . . ." He leaned over and placed both his hands over mine. "The thing is, you're a thoroughbred and, uh, *velour*, well, it's a bit barnyard."

Was that a no?

"You're classier than," he fingered the material with distaste, "than Juicy Couture."

"But it's a designer and everything!" I was confused. Lisa should have warned me. Instead, she'd said that it really showed off my body. Clearly, I couldn't trust her judgment. Maybe Evan was right about her. Was she trying to sabotage us? Was she jealous of me?

"You're my girl now, right?" He winked. "You've got to dress the part."

So it *was* true! I had heard that right! I was his girl!

"I'll even go shopping with you, if you want," he said. "I'd like to see you modelling new clothes . . . just for me."

I felt myself start to blush. It was my turn to examine my empty cup. Shopping required money and I didn't—

"What's wrong, did I embarrass you?" he asked.

I shook my head. "It's just with the play and cutting down my hours at the bakery . . . I just don't have . . ."

"It will be my treat," he said.

"I can't let you do that. You already pay for *everything*."

"A man is supposed to pay for his date. Call me old-fashioned, but that's the way I am. Can't a guy get his girl a present?"

His girl. He'd said it again. It was better each time.

"Consider it an early birthday present," he said.

"But my birthday isn't for months."

"Hence the *early* part." He paused. "It would be rude to turn down a present." He flashed that smile and my feet practically melted. "Okay?"

I nodded.

"Good." He got up, and right there in the coffee shop he bent down and kissed me. A lot of kids from school were still there. That sort of thing weirded me out a bit. I just wasn't used to being kissed in public, or to being kissed period, which must have been why it felt so intense or something. Lisa said that he was addicted to PDAs, public displays of affection. She was definitely jealous.

"Let's set a date and time," he said.

Everyone was looking. "But, I work remember, and then there's the play and homework. I don't know when we can go." That hadn't come out right, but Evan still smiled at me. He was so patient with me, and I was such a dork.

"It's okay, I'll pick you up after your second shift on Saturday and we'll spend the rest of the day getting you a few things that are up to your new standard."

Then I remembered Lisa and Travis.

"Don't worry, I'll still get you home for a really early night. I know you'll be tired."

Saturday, Lisa and Travis were going to line up to get student tickets for a dinnertime jazz concert, and I'd made plans to join them for a set. I hadn't really seen them over the past couple of weeks. Maybe I could see them on Sunday instead. I'd make up something.

"Yeah, wow, brilliant!" I finally said. "I'd love that!"

He pulled me to my feet. "And then, as a bonus, we can get together on Sunday, and I'll help you run lines."

Did I nod? How did this happen? He was so amazing. How did someone like *me* get someone like *him*? I must have said that last bit out loud.

"Stop that." He pulled me into him. "Repeat after me."

We were standing up together in the middle of the coffee shop. I felt singled out, like being on stage but different.

"Repeat after me," I repeated, and he poked me.

"I am special," he said.

"You *are* special." I giggled.

He poked me again, this time harder, much harder, and then repeated, slowly. "I am special—say it." It wasn't a request.

"I am special," I said.

"*You* made me special," he said.

"*You* made me special." I giggled again, but I believed it. He had made me special.

"So, I am special!" he said.

"So, I *am* special!" I said.

"There!" He squeezed. "I just saw you blossom right in front of me."

"Well, you're a good gardener." I squeezed his hand and noticed the time on his wristwatch.

"Yikes, its late, I've got to get my special blossoming butt home before my mom gets there!"

Evan glanced back at the room. "Okay, we can go now." Most of the kids were still looking but pretending not to. "I'll drop you off, my blossoming little rose." And then my prince actually kissed my hand. I could hear every girl in the place sighing. And so could he.

Chapter Twenty

Travis looked anxiously at his watch. Rehearsal should have started fifteen minutes ago, but Josh hadn't arrived. It made it hard to have a full practice with the lead actor not present.

I sat off to the side in one of the seats. I guess I could have gone backstage and helped Danny, but he seemed to be doing pretty well without my help. Set design—actually, anything involving tools or manual labour—wasn't really something I was any good at. And as my father always said, if you earned enough money it was easy to hire somebody to do that sort of thing.

"Could I please have your attention!" Ms. Cooper yelled as she came into the auditorium. "Could we have all the backstage people come out here as well!"

This sounded important. Well, as important as anything about this play could be. Slowly I got up from my seat and joined in with the crowd that was forming around her at the front of the stage. Katie settled in beside me. I slipped my hand into hers and I could feel her warmth.

"What do you think this is about?" she whispered.

I leaned in close. "Maybe Shakespeare called and said we couldn't do the play."

"No, seriously."

"I seriously don't have any idea . . . but Cooper doesn't look too happy."

"I want to start off by saying that he is going to be all right," Ms. Cooper began.

The level of tension in the room suddenly rose. Who was going to be all right?

"You'll all notice that Josh isn't here," she continued. "Because as we speak he is still in the Emergency Department of Credit Valley Hospital."

Stunned gasps and muffled shrieks shot around the stage.

"What happened?" Travis demanded.

"At lunch he was involved in a car accident. He's going to be fine, but the airbag of his car deployed and it broke his nose and jaw."

More gasps and groans from around the room.

"But what about the play?" Danny asked. "If his jaw is broken then they'll have to wire it shut, so there's no way he can say his lines."

"They did wire it shut," Ms. Cooper acknowledged.

"Are we going to have to cancel the play?" Travis asked.

"The show must go on."

"So we'll delay . . . wait for him to recover?" Travis questioned.

"It will be weeks before they remove the wires, and we can't wait that long," Ms. Cooper said. "Josh has to be replaced."

"Replaced?" Travis gasped. "But opening night isn't that far away. December 10 is going to be here before you know it!" Travis started pacing. "There's no way we can find somebody who can learn the lines in that time."

"We already have somebody who knows most of the lines," Cooper said.

I felt a chill go through me as I instantly I knew who she meant, and judging from how everybody turned to face me, they all knew too.

"Well, Evan?" Cooper asked. "You're the only chance we have."

I knew she was right.

"It's such short notice that I won't force you to do it if you don't want to," she said.

"So I can say no if I want?" I asked.

She nodded.

I let the question just hang in the air as everybody continued to stare at me. It looked like they were all almost afraid to breathe, waiting, anticipating, wondering what I was going to say. I liked keeping them waiting. It was like I had them all in the palm of my hand, like I was in total control of all of them . . . and really . . . I was.

I looked over at Katie. She looked like she was going to cry. I knew how much this play meant to her, and how much it would destroy her if it didn't go on.

"Of course I'll do it."

A cheer went up, and Katie threw her arms around me. I hugged her back as the rest of the cast and crew surrounded me, slapping me on the back and offering thanks.

I looked through the crowd to where Lisa sat in the seats a few rows back. She didn't look happy. Puzzled. That was it, she still looked at me like she was trying to figure me out. I guess it could have been worse—she could have *already* figured me out.

Chapter Twenty-One

I t was like God was trying to make up for every lousy little thing all in one go. Evan Campbell, the love of my life, was not only the love of my life, now he was also my Petruchio! Maybe Evan wasn't the most natural actor in the world, but I had a Petruchio who knew how to deliver lines, had them down cold AND actually knew what they meant. Ms. Cooper said that that fact alone put us ahead of 95 percent of all high school Shakespeare productions in the country.

Poor Josh. He was still at home sipping shakes because of the wires. Evan sent flowers on behalf of both of us. Like, wow. And that was exactly what I meant about him. I would never have thought of sending flowers, and even if I had, I wouldn't have known how to go about it. Evan did it all on his iPhone in less than a minute. He has his *own* florist! Like I said, wow. Don't get me wrong. I felt awful about Josh. We all did. Well, maybe not Travis. Travis looked relieved pretty much every time Evan opened his mouth and delivered a line. .

The only one who didn't like Evan taking Josh's place was Lisa. She'd been late for the first practice with him and now, for the second, she'd barely shown at all. Lisa was officially our prompter. It was going to say so on the playbill and everything. When Cooper dogged on her, Lisa said that Evan knew the script better than she did, and that I didn't "need her" any more. Cooper shamed her into promising to be a more prompt prompter. I didn't care. Okay, I did, but not enough. I was starting to get tired of her being so moody.

Travis was cool. Of course, Evan getting the lead, plus being my boyfriend, was seriously perfect for his play. But, unlike Lisa, I also think that Travis *got* that I was delirious, crazy, happy. Or he would have got it, if he hadn't been so preoccupied with the play.

When "we" sent the flowers to Josh, Evan asked what my favourite flowers were. Like, who does that?

Thing was, I didn't know. No one had ever asked.

He didn't laugh when I told him that. He just hugged me. Right there onstage after everyone had gone. Evan said to think about it. "It has to be some really special flower, Katie." Then he kissed me on the forehead. "Because you're special, remember?"

I would have followed that boy into battle.

I was still feeling pretty special as I ran up the eleven flights rather than wait for the elevator in our building. And I was special while I coated chicken legs in the dinky plastic bag they give you with the Shake'N Bake. When the front door slammed hard, I threw the legs into the oven while turning on the tap to rinse a head of iceberg lettuce. All of a sudden, I wasn't so special.

"Hey, good timing, Mom, just making the salad here!" I cranked up the oven to 500. "It'll be done in a sec!"

Mom came into the kitchen and went straight for the scotch cupboard. She drinks twelve-year-old Chivas Regal now. It's $63.95. Johnnie Walker scotch is $44.95, almost twenty dollars cheaper. That's what Mom drank before Nick Kormos introduced her to Chivas. Joey just drinks wine, expensive wine and lots of it, but he buys it and brings it.

I reached in for some ice and plopped it into her glass with my best "good daughter" smile. I was thinking maybe I should tell her about Evan. She'd for sure be impressed by his money, the car, his clothes, by so much.

Mom knocked the drink back in one go and poured another while eyeing me.

"What the hell you grinning at?"

Okay, so we'd save Evan for another time. I knew better than to answer. It was like walking on a razor's edge when she was like this. She knocked back the second scotch and kept eyeing me.

"That outfit is too tight on you, makes you like you're selling something," she snapped.

Wow, and this from someone who wore gold lamé tank tops. That snide little thought was immediately replaced by the deeply uncomfortable realization that I must have had *her* taste in clothes.

"You think you're smarter than me. But you're not," she said. Mom poured another scotch and got her own ice cubes. I braced myself by chopping the red peppers and green onions for the salad. I needed to be invisible. To not react. To keep my mouth shut.

"You think I can't see those little wheels turning in your head. You can shut up all you want, but I know what you're thinking. You're just like your dad, your useless, limp father!"

I nicked my finger and it started bleeding on the lettuce so I held it under the running water. Now we had pink lettuce. My back was to her.

"Don't think I don't know that you're saying stuff about me in your head. You got a smart mouth in your head." I heard her snort and then gulp. "You think you'll fake me out by keeping your mouth shut."

She was scary like that, she just knew stuff in a wild, feral kind of way. You couldn't keep secrets from my mother.

I gripped the counter and braced for the inevitable. Nothing. My blood continued dribbling freely into the sink. Then I heard a familiar catch in her breath. I turned around. Sure enough, tears streamed down my mother's face.

"What, Mom, what is it?" She let loose then. My mother cried like her world had disintegrated. "What, Mommy? Tell me! Are you okay? Is it Joey? What, Mommy, what?"

"He didn't return my calls today. I left messages . . ."

"He's probably just busy. You know how busy Joey is."

Her body convulsed. "They all leave!" she sobbed. "I'm sorry, so sorry baby, sorry . . ."

About what? My breath snagged on a piece of broken glass. My life would not be worth living if Joey had dumped her.

"Has Joey . . . has he broken . . . ?"

"No." She shook her head. "Not yet."

Stuff was coming out of her nose, her mascara ran in rivers down her cheeks and she was heaving uncontrollably. "But it's just a matter of time. They all leave! Why wouldn't they? Why would anyone stay with a piece of garbage like me? I make myself sick! Oh, Jesus!"

I threw my arms around her. My mother was smaller than me. When had that happened?

"Stop! Don't! Please, don't!" I cried.

I couldn't bear the sounds coming out of her little body and I couldn't stop the tears coming out of mine. The howls of grief shook through her and straight into me. I was useless. I usually was. The sound of her crying petrified me. It was always like that. Somehow my mother's tears made the floors and the walls disappear. It made me feel like I was hanging unsupported in a dark room. But I held on to her and we rocked, clinging to each other and waiting out the storm.

Every so often Mom would let go for a bit and look at me all confused. Once I saw a flash of hurt—or was it guilt?—but it disappeared before I could be sure whether I had really seen it or just wished it there. And still she cried. About what? I shivered and held her tighter. Nothing made me more lonely than seeing my mother cry.

"Please, Mommy, don't worry. Joey loves you. I know that. Please stop, you're so special and so, so beautiful. Everyone says."

"They do?" That caught her. She reached for a kitchen towel and blew her nose. "They say I'm beautiful?"

"Always!" I nodded. "You'll see, if you come to opening night, everyone will hardly notice me, they'll all be looking at you."

She blew again. "You think?"

"Absolutely, for sure, Mom."

She'd stopped. It was finished.

"I could've modelled, you know?" she said.

"But Daddy wouldn't let you because you had me and everything." I held my breath. This could go one of two ways.

"That's right. That man said I could have been a model."

It was like she was nodding to someone sitting across from her at the table. She let the after-sobbing tremors ripple through her body, and then my mom stood up. She was done, but I didn't want to let her go.

"I'm going to lie down for a minute." Mom headed out of the kitchen.

I missed her already.

She turned and leaned into the doorway. "Don't think I don't know what you're doing. I'm *still* the smart one here, the one with the power."

"Okay, Mom. That's right. You'll feel a lot better after a little nap. You're just tired is all."

"Shut up!" She stared at me like I was some intruder who had broken into her kitchen. "I know what you're up to. If you think you can out-manipulate me, you've got another thing coming. You don't have an ounce of *me* in you. You, Katie, are 100 percent your deadbeat dad. I look at you and see him. Look at you, now," she snorted. "Some actress you're going to be." And with that she swayed off to her room.

Some part of me had known it was coming, all of it. And yes, I remembered. In the end, there was an order: Act One, inconsolable, heart-shredding tears; Act Two, hugging and healing; and then Act Three, recriminations, shame about the first two acts. Mom always felt bad about needing me, afterwards. It was a three-act, three-scotch scenario. It had played out like clockwork, and yet I'd still been taken by surprise. Special? Yeah, I was especially stupid. Still, as gutted as I was at the end of the performance, it was worth acting out the whole thing just for those few minutes of holding and being held by her.

I stood in the middle of the kitchen, my finger still bleeding on the towel she'd used to wipe her nose. What a play. What an act.

I bowed to my audience of no one.

Chapter Twenty-Two

"Dinner was so wonderful," Katie said. "Thank you for having me."

"It was our pleasure. It was wonderful to meet you," my father answered, charmingly.

He'd been on his best "we have company, people are watching" type of behaviour. He could be the most charming person in the world when he wanted to be. That charm had served him so well.

"I'm so happy to have had the chance to meet you," Katie said. "Both of you," she said, turning to my mother to include her in the conversation.

"It was such a joy for us to meet you," my mother sang out—and I knew she meant it.

"Yes, a *real* joy," my father agreed.

From him, that might have been the truth or it might have been a lie. You could never tell—at least not from his tone or words or expression. You just had to *know*. Sometimes I could read him, but this time I couldn't. But why wouldn't he like Katie?

"It's rare for my son to invite his friends over these days," my father said.

I didn't say anything. He should have known why that was.

"In fact, I expect he thought I wouldn't even be here today," he added. "I wasn't scheduled to be home until the middle of next week."

I tried to keep my face neutral. He was right.

"But I was able to successfully conclude my business in Tokyo earlier than expected . . . have you ever been to Japan?"

"I can only dream about going someplace like that," Katie said.

"It's good to have a dream," he said. "Well, I'm not going to bore you all with the details of my business transactions, but they were very, shall we say, productive and lucrative."

I knew he was now going to go ahead and bore us with the details, and sure enough he started throwing out numbers and names. There were three of us listening—or in my case pretending to listen—but this story was aimed at an audience of one: Katie. He always needed to do that with new people. Not because they were important, just because he liked having a brand-new audience to dazzle. Like a reason to climb a mountain, she was just there.

I looked over at Katie. She looked captivated by his story, even though she probably didn't have the capacity to understand the complexities of the deal he was describing. What mattered was the masterful way he was spinning his tale, painting himself as some sort of emperor of high finance. I'd seen this act so many times before.

"So what does your father do?" he asked.

"I have no idea," Katie said. "I don't really know him."

"Oh . . . that's . . . unfortunate."

A deadly silence filled the room.

"I'll just clear off the table and then bring out dessert," my mother said, getting to her feet.

"Let me help you with the dishes," Katie said as she got up too.

"That's not necessary," my father said. "You're our guest."

"No, I want to help."

The two of them gathered the plates and then left, the door to the kitchen swinging closed behind them, leaving us alone.

"It's obvious that your new school's lower academic standards also apply to the quality of its dating pool," my father said in a low voice.

"What?"

"Well, really, how would you compare her to Sarah?"

Sarah was a former girlfriend—not the last one, but the one he liked to use as the gold standard against which all other girls were measured.

"I don't compare them," I said.

"You're probably wise. It would be like comparing diamonds to rhinestones."

"That's not fair!"

"You're right. Rhinestones at least have some glitter. I'll just have to assume this girl must be very good in the sack," he said.

"What?"

"Well, why else would you be dating her? I'm just looking for a reason."

"I'm not going to talk to you about this."

"Which must mean there *is* something to talk about," he said. "Just make sure you're using protection."

"I'm *not* sleeping with her."

"That's probably better. Fewer complications. The last thing you want is to get somebody like *that* pregnant."

"What is that supposed to mean—somebody like *that*?"

"Isn't it obvious? I just don't see it, that's all I'm saying. You have to understand that dating and marriage are simply a reflection of the two parties' respective market values."

"Everything comes down to a price with you, doesn't it?"

He shook his head slowly and his expression was one of disgust . . . no, disappointment . . . disappointment in me. I knew that look well enough.

"Everything *does* come down to a price. The market value of each person is made up of the sum of their parts," he said.

"You're making this sound like a real estate deal."

"That's good, because it really is no different from a real estate deal. Finding valid market value, determining how much money a residence is worth—it's based on the components of that property. Location, size, features. With a person, you look at things like physical appearance, education, occupation or future occupation, future potential as a wage-earner, status of parents and their economic position, personalities, friends, activities, etc. You give each component a weighted value—for example, physical appearance is more significant for a female—and then add up all the variables. Your Katie is beautiful enough, but low-rent in every other way. It's all a simple formula, and people tend to date and then marry partners of equal market value."

"How romantic."

"Romance is for idiots."

"Love plays no role in any of this?" I questioned.

"Are you saying you're in love with her?" he asked, as though he couldn't believe either his ears or the idea itself.

I didn't answer right away, but I could tell by his expression that he needed an answer.

"No, of course not."

"Good. I didn't think so. Although I could see where she might fall in love with you." He paused. "Or at least think she's in love with you because of your higher market value. You'd be a big step up for her."

"Shall I take that as a personal compliment?" I asked.

"It says as much about your family as it does about you. This house, your car, the money, the status all are part of *your* increased market value."

"So you're saying she might fall in love with me, but it would be, at least in part, because of *you* and what you provide?"

"Of course I'm part of it. Regardless, you shouldn't take any of this as a compliment so much as a warning."

"A warning about what?"

"Don't let yourself get trapped. The best way for a female to gain status is to marry up, and the best way to do that is to get pregnant. You don't think that girl hasn't looked around this house and seen there's money here?"

"That's ridiculous."

"Is it?"

"If this is such a problem, why weren't you warning me about Sarah trapping me?" I asked.

"I think that's something her parents were warning *her* about."

A cheap shot. Not unexpected, but it still hurt. I wasn't going to let him see that, though.

"I guess you're right," I agreed, straining to sound completely calm. "After all, her father does earn a lot more money than you."

I saw a slight reaction in his face. Hitting him in the wallet was where it hurt him the most. Maybe he didn't have a heart or soul, but he did have a bank account and that was how he measured himself as a man.

"Your status certainly hasn't improved by being asked to leave your last school," he said, firing back at me.

"If you had really wanted me to stay you could have fought harder for me," I said.

"There was no point. It was simply an embarrassment that I didn't need."

"How about what I needed?"

"Are you deliberately trying to get me angry?" he hissed.

I saw that look in his eyes. I'd pushed—maybe too far. "No . . . no, sir."

"Good. It's time you stopped whining and complaining and started to act like a man. Take control over yourself and control of those around you. Be a man and—"

"That sounds like a very serious conversation," my mother said as she came back into the room, carrying a tray filled with desserts, followed by Katie.

"It was serious," my father said.

My mother skidded to a stop. She now looked concerned and a bit worried. "Do you want us to leave you alone to continue your discussion?"

"Of course not, my dear," he said, his voice suddenly soft and friendly again. He rose to his feet and took the tray from her—now all charm and courtly manners. "No discussion, no matter how serious, should be continued when we have the opportunity to spend time with two such lovely young ladies!"

It was like turning on a tap. He was all smiles.

My mother giggled—a nervous release from the tension she was feeling—and Katie blushed. I liked when she blushed so much. I liked lots of things about her. Not that there wasn't room for change or—

"Evan and I will have lots of time to discuss things further after our guest leaves," my father said.

The smile was still on his lips, but there was an ominous tone—one that Katie wouldn't even have noticed. But I had. And so had my mother.

Chapter Twenty-Three

❤

I didn't get it. I didn't get how anyone who had a house like that could be with someone like me. Evan's house was beyond the beyond and then some.

Lisa lived in a huge, expensive place too—it looked like it was set in a park. I didn't have the words to describe the architecture, but it was covered in dirty old stone and had a slate roof with lots of pretty points. It was for sure exactly what you'd think of if someone told you to close your eyes tight and then said, "Quick, think mansion!"

But Evan's—Evan's house was all boxes and right angles, glass on glass, tubular steel and concrete, inside and out, except that inside, there were leather places to sit . . . if you dared—white-on-white leather.

I'd never been so scared of a hallway in my life. As soon as we stepped in and started to cross the polished stone floors, Evan put his hand protectively behind my back. I loved it when he did that. It filled me up and made me brave.

"Well, what do you think?" he whispered.

"Oh my God, Evan, I don't know. It's like a very, very expensive IKEA store."

He didn't stop laughing until his father came out to greet us. I am such an idiot. I don't even know why what I said was funny.

Evan was surprised to see his dad walk over to us, I could tell. I was surprised too. Evan had told me it was just going to be his mother, because his father was supposed to be still away. So it was just lucky for me that I got to meet the both of them. Mr. Campbell was very handsome. Well, not as handsome as Joey, Mom's silver fox, but distinguished-looking handsome. And so was she. Mrs. Campbell, I mean. Mom would have said there wasn't an ounce of fat on her and that she could've actually used a pound here and there. Mom also liked to say that a man likes to have something to hang on to, when all is said and done. But let's face it, the Campbells were a whole different class of people, and who knew what they liked?

"Well, what is so funny? Do share," said Mr. Campbell, reaching for my hand.

My heart stopped. What if Evan told him about the IKEA thing? I'd already figured out that it must have been a massively insulting comparison, even though I had said "very, very expensive."

"Katie is always making me laugh, Dad."

I shook Mr. Campbell's hand and then Evan's mother's—she was just a foot or two behind him.

"You'll see. It's one of the reasons I love her."

Love her? *Love her?* Evan said "love her." Did he mean me? What did he mean, exactly? I kept smiling and nodding as we went into a blindingly white living room, but I was parsing his words, which were still in the hallway. Was it like "You gotta love her" *or* "Mum, Dad, this is Katie Rosario and I love her"? The only thing that snapped me out of it was when Mrs. Campbell offered me a pomegranate juice concoction. Dear God, sipping Perrier in this room would have made me nervous. Pomegranate? Really? And to top it off, the crystal glass felt paper-thin. I cupped it like it was the

Holy Grail. It was only when I was seated that I noticed that not all of the white sofas and pillows were pure white. Close up I could see that some things were actually covered in a creamy or off-white silk fabric.

"Thank you for inviting me to your beautiful home, Mrs. Campbell." She caught me staring at the pillow closest to my drink in abject terror.

"It's dupioni silk, my dear. Lovely, isn't it?"

"Oh, yes, of course. It's so lovely." I was frantically mirroring her every gesture and now tried to get her "tone" right. Mrs. Campbell smiled. Okay, so far, so good.

"I imagine that Shakespeare's Katherina may even have worn dupioni," Mrs. Campbell said.

"Well, she may have," I agreed. It was nice of her to bring up the play. "But I have a feeling the school budget won't allow for Katherina to be smothered in silk."

"That's a shame. I'm sure that you would look splendid draped in full-on dupioni." Was she mocking me? My mom would have had a field day with "a little dupioni for my little dope," or something. No, Evan's mom was still smiling at me.

"Philip and I are so looking forward to the production. Evan hasn't been in a play since middle school. And you're so strong and beautiful, my dear, you'll look wonderful in whatever they concoct for you. The perfect Kate!"

I *loved* this woman.

Okay, so, dinner was different. It was like I'd been raised in a cave until that night. We had this flat white fish that wasn't covered in batter and didn't have a drop of cream of tartar sauce. We also had this sweet potato and quinoa combo that Mrs. Campbell had "picked up" at Whole Foods, along with a spinach and mushroom salad. I didn't have a clue what "quinoa" was. It was all good, I guess, except I was still hungry.

All through dinner, Mr. Campbell told us—but it was really like he was just telling me—all about his latest business "transactions." The way he told it, he got on and off planes the way I rode the subway. He had just returned from Tokyo that day! Japan! He made it all sound so glamorous and funny. Sounded like you practically had to take your shoes off just to order tea over there. He was so patient about explaining the business terms to me. I almost understood what he was talking about. Now I could see where Evan got his gift.

Then he asked about my father. I don't remember what I said, but I'm sure it was stupid. All I know is that I jumped up and the next thing I knew I was scraping off plates with Mrs. Campbell in their stainless-steel kitchen, and I mean that—all of the appliances, and even the backsplash, were stainless steel. I could hardly wait to tell my mom, or better yet Joey—he would have been so impressed.

I winced. I hadn't even told Mom about Evan yet. She'd been so busy with Joey and, let's face it, with avoiding me. Mom always avoided me for weeks after one of her crying jags. They were going away again the next day. Well, at least we argued a lot less when she wasn't around to argue with.

I could feel Mrs. Campbell sneaking looks at me as I scraped, rinsed and stacked.

"Evan tells me that you do all of the cooking at your house." She was rinsing raspberries. "Not that I cook, per se . . ."

"Oh, you're a great cook," I lied. "Like that fish thing you did. I wouldn't know how to do that. I just do your basic thaw and serve and then throw the Kraft's Thousand Island on some lettuce kind of stuff. But it keeps us going, and I like to learn. Like, weirdly enough, Joey can cook. That's Mom's boyfriend. He's famous. He's on concrete benches all over the city. Anyway, Joey cooks with real ingredients, fresh and everything, and I sort of pay attention to what he's doing."

Mrs. Campbell just kept smiling.

"I wish I knew how to do that spinach salad thing that you picked up at the . . ."

"Whole Foods."

"Right." I still didn't know if that was a store or a restaurant.

"I hate to disillusion you, because I'm basking in the way you look at me, Katie, but I don't know what they do either. Your mother must be very proud of you."

Oh yeah. . . . Wait, she wasn't trying to be funny. I chopped faster.

"Evan tells me that not only are you the lead in the play, but you work double shifts at a bakery, stay on the honour roll, and you make dinner every night. That is a considerable feat."

Wow. What was it with these people? Wait! Evan talked about me! To his mother! And now she was talking to me like I mattered. What a family! If I ever had kids, I was going to raise them exactly the same way, telling them how great they were—whether they were or not.

"Well, dinner is all about eating, right? And the honour roll isn't that impressive. I mean, I used to think so until I met Evan, and now I know what a real education and real smarts are."

She walked up behind me and gently turned me around. "Don't sell yourself short, Katie. You start now and you'll never stop. It's . . . addictive." Her eyes clouded and somehow she looked a little less skinny right then. "Okay!" She cleared up. "Let's get this to the men." She slid the raspberries and sliced strawberries into some other mystery fruit, picked up the bowl and went back into the dining room. I took a last quick glance around that shiny, shiny, kitchen. What had just happened?

Mr. Campbell and Evan both looked a little guilty when we got back. Evan actually stood up and held the chair for his mother, then me. I mean, if I hadn't loved him already I'd have tumbled right then and there!

Before Mrs. Campbell started spooning out the fruit thingy—if that was dessert, no wonder she was so skinny—she reached over and placed her hand over mine and looked directly at Evan. "I am so happy that you brought Katie home to meet us, dear. It's going to be a real pleasure getting to know her better."

Mr. Campbell raised his glass and said, "Hear, hear." He winked at me.

It was practically the best night of my life. How sweet were they? How beautiful and glamorous and smart and nice! No wonder Evan was exactly the way he was!

Chapter Twenty-Four

"Tramp!" Mom slapped me so hard the keys dropped out of my hand and onto the floor. "Where have you been, you tramp?"

"What? Ow! Mom!" I bent over to retrieve the keys. "What are you doing here?" I gasped.

"We're going to go in the morning," she said, now calm after the storm. But she still stepped towards me, pushing my back into the door. "Where were you?" She exhaled and finally stepped away. "It's almost midnight. I know you have to be in bed early because of the bakery. Where the hell were you?" She took a few deep breaths. "Your little friend Lisa left a message. Wondering if you had any time to get together because she *misses* you and apologizes for being such a pill about *Evan*." Mom made a face on the "misses" part. "So don't bother with some garbage about being with your friends. I know you only have her and the queer."

"Travis is, well, not for sure anyway . . ."

I heard the toilet flush. Of course Joey would be here. He came out into the living room still zipping up his pants. He took us both in and killed his smile.

"There *is* somebody, Mom, and I've been wanting to tell you," I said.

I could see her breath quickening again. What was up? I glanced over at the dining room table. The empty plates and glasses were still there. They'd killed a couple of bottles of wine, but I didn't see the scotch out.

"You'd like him, he's really rich."

"Then what's he doing with you? Milking the cow, I suspect."

"Cheryl!" That was Joey. He looked at Mom like he'd never seen her before.

"He is NOT like that! Evan is a gentleman and he *loves* me. He even said so in front of his parents!" Okay, not really, but sort of.

"You met the folks, kid?" said Joey. "Hey, that's a real promising sign. Where do they live?"

"On Hawkins Avenue, off Richard Street."

Joey let out a long, slow whistle. "What number?"

"I don't know. It's big and it's like a bunch of boxes that—"

"The mid-century modern, number 72?" He whistled again. "Those types move around a lot, maybe you can introduce me."

That would've been an unbearably Joey-like comment to make, except that I knew in my gut that he was trying to deflect Mom.

"I told them about you already," I said, all proud of myself. "I said that was you on all the benches!"

Joey smiled his big bus shelter smile. "Thanks, kid."

"And his dad just got back from Tokyo, and his mom is so sweet and beautiful—"

"And I ask again!" It was too much for Mom. She, of course, took a compliment about anybody as an insult to her. I saw it instantly, right then. Looking from Joey to her, I saw what she saw. It wasn't just in her head. My mom's radar was brilliant and unerring. She was losing Joey. Joey didn't even know it yet.

But Mom did.

"So, I ask, what does a boy like that want with a little *tramp* like you? Ooops, or did I just stumble onto the answer?"

"I *said* he's not like that, Mom! Evan pays for everything and opens the door and tells me about fajitas and artichokes . . ." My cheek was still throbbing from her slap. "And he's my Petruchio, and he's so smart!" I was sucking back furious tears. "And he would never . . . because he is such a gentleman! Not that someone like you would ever know about gentlemen!" I paused as I realized what I'd just said. "No offence, Mr. Campana."

"None taken, kid." He shrugged. "And call me Joey!"

"Look you snivelling little—"

"Cheryl, for godsake!"

Joey took my mom by the arm and led her into the bedroom, said something to her and shut the door. Then he trotted back to where I was still standing, in the middle of the living room, one hand holding my keys and the other holding my cheek.

"Look, kid . . ." He was whispering and looking at the floor with a fair degree of intensity. "Your mom's had a bit too much to drink. She'll be right as rain by the time we get back, I promise. She loves ya to pieces." He looked up and winked. "Go to bed and forget about all of this. Didn't happen. Okay?"

I nodded. My humiliated heart bristled with gratitude. Joey had saved me from her. For the hundredth time I vowed that I was done with my mom. I would never care again. My mother was old, this was over, and she was angry because she knew it.

"Okay," I said.

Joey gave me a thumbs-up sign, then he turned around and went back to her.

It was exactly 12:30 a.m. I had to get up in three hours.

I went to my room. Evan had said he loved me. He'd said that

I always made him laugh, and that was one of the reasons he *loved* me. Okay, even if he didn't mean it in *that* way, he *did* love me. Maybe he didn't know it yet, but I did.

I looked at the phone. My cheek still throbbed. She packed a hell of a hit for such a little thing. I shut the door and pressed the message button and listened while I changed.

You have one message:
Hey Katie, Katie, it's Lisa. Hey girl, I'm sorry, I've been in
kind of a snit, not coming to rehearsals to help you out and
just be around for you . . . yeah. And well, sorry, I've been
a bit of a dick about Evan too, I guess. Never mind why,
doesn't matter. I uh, well, I miss you and I know you're real
busy with the play and well, Evan, etc., but I'm here and I'll
always be right here. Okay? Yeah, so how about a frappuccino
on Sunday? Whether you've got any time or not, we're friends
for life, got it? Not the normal kind, in the normal way, but
friends for life. I mean it. Love ya, later.

Love ya? Love *me*? Wow. People were lining up in droves to love me. I turned off the light: 12:33 a.m. Why didn't I feel any of it?

Chapter Twenty~Five

I looked back at my car, parked on the road in front of the building, wondering if it would be safe there. Maybe, maybe not, but really, what did I care? Any damage done would just be an expense my father would have to absorb. Maybe I could damage it myself. Hitting him in the wallet was the place that hurt. And I wanted to hurt him.

I shifted the flowers and presents into one hand as I opened the door to the lobby, and then caught a wave of, ugh . . . what was that smell? Had somebody died in here or . . . ? No . . . not died . . . relieved themselves.

The carpet was ratty, the paint chipped and the board listing the tenants was scratched and worn. Some of the names were blank, others unreadable, others were unrecognizable. I knew she was in apartment 911, but I had to buzz up to have her let me in and I couldn't see what number to buzz.

"Are you going up?"

I looked over. It was an old woman—a *really* old woman—and she was coming out of the building, still holding the door.

"Yes . . . thanks," I said as I headed for the door.

"Just hold on a second." She held the door but stood blocking the opening. "Who are you here to visit?" she asked.

"My girlfriend."

"And you don't know her code?"

"I've always gone in with her," I lied. "I've never had to buzz up to go to her apartment . . . she's in 911."

She nodded her head and I gave her a big smile.

"We're really not supposed to hold the door for people we don't know," she said.

"I appreciate you letting me in."

She chuckled. "And I don't normally let just anybody in, but you don't look like no thief."

"I'm not," I assured her.

She went out as I went in. One of the elevators was waiting, the door open. I climbed in and pushed floor nine. The door slid shut, sealing me inside with a smell that wasn't much better than the lobby's, and it lurched upward. I looked around at the graffiti, scratched into the walls and written with black marker. Other than the quantity there was nothing impressive or creative. At the ninth floor the door opened—an inch below the level of the floor. I stepped up and out. Left or right. I went to the right—fifty-fifty chance.

The colour and pattern of the rug in the hallway didn't match the lobby's, but the worn and ratty feeling was consistent. So was the peeling paint. I passed by apartments, each with its own sick sounds and smells spilling out.

When I got to 911 I listened at the door before knocking. I couldn't hear anything, but she had to be back from work . . . unless she'd gone out right after? Unless she was with somebody else? It was hard not knowing where she was, but soon that wasn't going to be a problem, because I'd always know where she was.

I knocked and I heard somebody moving around inside. Then a shadow appeared at the little peephole in the door, instantly followed by the sound of a chain being pulled across. The door swung open.

"Evan, what are you doing here?" Katie said. Her tone was hesitant, worried, concerned. Was there somebody in there with her?

"I wanted to surprise you," I said. I wondered just how surprised we were both going to be.

"You did surprise me, but you should have called!"

"Then it wouldn't have been a surprise. Are you going to invite me in?"

"Of course. It's just that the place is a mess. *I'm* a mess."

"I didn't come to see the place, and you look wonderful. As wonderful as these." I handed her the flowers.

"For me?"

I laughed. "I almost had to give them to an old woman in the lobby as the price of admission, but they're for you. They're your favourite flowers."

"My favourite?" she exclaimed as she started to undo the wrapping. "I don't really have a favourite." She pulled the flowers out of the paper. "They're beautiful . . . wow."

"They're orchids. Your new favourite flowers are expensive and exotic. Rare and beautiful. Like you."

I saw her just melt in front of my eyes. I loved it when she did that. I've known so many girls who would have faked appreciation for the flowers but waited for something more—something more expensive. She was blown away by the flowers—and really, if they'd only been daisies that I'd picked from the front lawn she would have felt the same.

"So, are you going to let me all the way in or do I have to stand in the hall?"

"I'm sorry . . . sorry . . . of course . . . the flowers . . . !"

She took my hand and led me down the dim hallway—was there a light bulb out or something? She brought me into the living room.

There were a couple of couches, a La-Z-Boy chair and a coffee table with dozens of cup rings marring the top. I could see where that IKEA comment had come from, because IKEA would have been a big step up. In the corner was a flat-screen TV—about the only thing worth anything in the whole place.

"Just have a seat while I put these in water and get freshened up a little," she said.

"The flowers can wait, and maybe I like the smell of baked goods. Come and sit down."

"But—"

"That *wasn't* a request." I took her by the hand and pulled her down to sit beside me on the couch. It creaked under our weight.

"First off, is your mother home?"

She shook her head.

"Is she going to be home soon?"

"She's gone for the weekend."

"That's too bad. I was hoping to meet her." I paused. "But . . . since we're alone." I pulled the bottle of Dwersteg from the bag. "I liberated it from my father's liquor cabinet. It's a liqueur . . . very tasty . . . it's a very exclusive coffee liqueur, like Bailey's or Kahlua but much, *much* better." And much more potent. "It's the perfect thing to celebrate your present."

"They *are* beautiful flowers," she said.

"They are, but they aren't the present. This is." I pulled the little box from the inner pocket of my jacket.

Katie gasped. "You really don't have to get me anything . . . anything more."

"I don't *have* to get you anything. I *wanted* to get you something. I'm afraid if you're my girl you're going to have to get used to getting presents."

She reached for the box and I pulled it back. "But first, go and get us a couple of glasses and fill them with ice. And hurry, before I change my mind."

She jumped to her feet and practically ran into the kitchen. I could hear the cupboard open, then the fridge, and then the unmistakable sound of clinking ice. Katie reappeared holding two glasses and placed them on the coffee table.

I undid the top of the bottle. "It's imported from Germany," I said as I started to pour it over the ice. "Organic, made from Arabica coffee beans."

"Coffee. I like coffee," Katie said. "I *love* frappuccinos."

"I know that." I handed her the glass. "To you," I said.

"To us."

We clinked our glasses together and she took a little sip. "This is good!"

"Did you expect me to give you something that tasted bad?"

"No, it's just that I didn't expect it to taste *this* good. I don't drink very much, and I didn't know that liquor could taste like this. This is delicious."

"Have some more," I said. I didn't wait for a response. I tipped the bottle and filled her glass to the top. "Now, for the present."

She took it from me. "It's so pretty," she said, admiring the wrapping.

"It's what's inside that matters."

Carefully she tried to undo the bow and remove the paper without ripping it.

"Just open it!" I yelled.

She ripped open the paper and—

"It's a phone!" she exclaimed.

"Not just a phone—it's the same as *my* phone. The best money can buy!"

She cradled it in her hands like it was a baby. "It's beautiful . . . it's wonderful . . . but . . ."

"And I prepaid a plan for the first six months, so don't worry about how you can afford it," I said.

"I don't know what to say."

"How about thank you?" I suggested.

"Thank you . . . thank you so much."

She wrapped her arms around me and gave me a big hug. I could feel her body pressed against me through the thin top she was wearing.

"I worry about you coming home alone late at night without me there to protect you. This way, I know you're going to be safe." It would also mean that I'd always know where she was and who she was with. Every minute, day or night.

"It's just that you give me so much, and I've never given you anything," she said.

"You give me more than you know," I said. But not nearly as much as she was going to give me, I thought. "Now go and get changed so I can start to show you how to use the apps," I said.

"I thought you liked the smell of baked goods," Katie said.

"The smell is beautiful, but I need you wearing something beautiful. I want a new picture of you to be the background on my phone. Every time I take out my phone I want to see you. Now, be a good little girl and go and get changed into something pretty."

"And you could be on *my* phone."

"I'm counting on that. Now get going," I said.

She got up.

"But wait!" I grabbed her by the arm. "Finish your drink first." I handed her the half-filled glass and then picked up mine. "Bottoms up."

We both drained our glasses until there was nothing left but the ice cubes.

"Now go. And remember . . . something pretty . . . and *sexy.*"

She blushed before she disappeared into her bedroom.

First thing, I refilled both glasses. A little alcohol could go a long way, and a lot of alcohol even further. Not that I was planning on going anywhere that night. Her mother wasn't coming back and I had already had too much to drink to even think about driving. The only question now was how far could I get Katie to go?

I looked around the apartment. It was nothing short of pathetic. Other than the flat-screen there wasn't one item that would ever have been allowed in my house. Actually, there wasn't really anything good enough to be found in the garbage in my neighbourhood.

I started to think about what my father had told me about market value. As much as I hated to admit it, I knew he was right. I had the house, the car, the look, the feel, the future, the status and the money. I certainly had so much more. Katie was going to have to compensate in other ways. That's what I was counting on.

I heard the door open and looked up. She was dressed in the outfit I'd guessed she'd be in—the one I'd bought her. Nice, low-cut top, and she was even wearing heels. I *loved* heels. She'd dabbed on some makeup and brushed out her hair. It didn't matter much because those weren't the areas I was going to be focusing on.

"Well?" she asked.

"Nice . . . very nice."

That word didn't even come close. She almost took my breath away. She was beautiful, and she didn't know it. Beautiful and innocent and grateful . . . and mine.

I looked around the apartment, searching for the best backdrop for a picture. There was no best place, only less-bad places. I took her by the hand and led her over to a simple blank wall.

"Now give me a smile," I said as I aimed the phone camera at her.

Katie smiled. A sweet little smile that said she wasn't just happy but grateful. And I knew, right then, that I could get her to do anything I wanted. Anything. And I started thinking that what she needed was to be protected, to be cared for. She was an innocent in a world filled with predators. All she wanted was somebody to care for her, to love her.

And then I remembered something my father always said—repeatedly, incessantly. It didn't matter if it was business or your personal life: either dominate or be dominated; either be in control or be controlled. Somebody was always up in every relationship and somebody was always down. And I wasn't going to be down—not again, not in this one.

"How are you feeling?" I asked.

"I think I'm a little woozy . . . a little drunk."

"Only a little? Here, have another drink."

I reached over and grabbed her glass from the table. She took it and tipped it back. Apparently I wasn't the only one who thought she needed more alcohol.

"Now, how about if we turn the heat up a little," I suggested. I reached over and undid her top two buttons.

She went to brush my hand away. "Evan . . . I don't know if—"

"I *do* know. It's just a shot for me. Something *just* for me. But if you're afraid or you don't trust me I can just leave, right now."

I started to get up and she reached over, taking my arm, stopping me.

"I don't want you to leave," she said.

"You can't have it both ways. Either you trust me or you don't."

"I trust you!"

"Then show me," I said. "Show me you trust me. Show me you love me . . . the way I love you."

"You love me?" she asked, her voice filled with doubt. "You really love me?"

"Don't be stupid." She winced. "Of course I love you. Don't you love me?"

She hesitated for a second and then her hands went up to her blouse. She undid the buttons all the way down until it hung open, revealing her lingerie underneath.

"Beautiful," I said as I clicked off a few pictures. "Now just a few more shots to let me know that you care for me the way I care for you . . . that you're mine."

She was mine—mine to control—and I'd have the evidence to prove that this time whatever happened was her idea, too, that it was voluntary. Nobody could say anything different.

"Now, how about going a little bit further," I suggested.

She hesitated. I knew she knew what I meant.

"For me," I said gently.

She gave me a smile . . . a sad little smile . . . and for a split second I thought better of what I was asking her to do, I felt bad.

And then she did what I'd asked.

All of it.

Chapter Twenty-Six

·♡·

I puked all day. Just when I thought that there was absolutely nothing left, not a thing more that could possibly come up, I'd barely make it to the bathroom and heave some more. I knew the drill, sort of. I'd watched and heard my mom go through this for as long as I could remember. Okay, well, not this bad for sure, but I had seen and cleaned "hangovers from hell," as she called them. I knew I'd survive, although for most of that day I wasn't sure I wanted to.

The next day would be the start of dress rehearsals. I didn't pick up my manuscript once. I didn't eat a single thing. I did shower—four times.

And I still felt dirty.

There were some marks on me, in places that I had to contort myself to see and some in more, uh, obvious places. I couldn't, wouldn't, remember what exactly, specifically, had happened, and any time I caught a flash of something, I winced so hard that my head erupted. I reeled with hurt, was dizzy with the betrayal. How could he? He was supposed to take care of me.

Was there a camera? Yes, on the phone. Evan had bought me a phone, but he'd also taken pictures of me with a different phone, his phone. He'd had me pose, lots of poses in . . . I winced again. I didn't know whether I felt more ashamed or angry. How dare he!

Righteous rage and shame battled it out while I listened to "The Hour of Power" from the Crystal Cathedral. Apparently Jesus forgave me. Jesus forgave everybody everything, so he had to forgive me for, for ... whatever had happened last night. I checked the time, 11:00 a.m. I was going to have to watch this show every Sunday from now on. I had a feeling I was going to need a lot of forgiving. Maybe Jesus would forgive Evan, too. I sure wouldn't, no way. *Just wait until he calls.*

I looked at my iPhone. It was already programmed and loaded with "all the apps I'd ever want." I didn't even know what apps I wanted. But Evan knew. He was amazing that way. He knew which clothes would look good on me, which colours. What my favourite flowers were.

I stumbled my way into the living room again. There they were. Yellow orchids. The smell almost knocked me flat. A cloying citrusy aroma danced around the Ajax that was still clinging to my hands from the last cleanup.

He'd said he loved me. It all came flooding back. How he'd taken more pictures. Just for him, to remind him of how hot I was. "You're so beautiful, baby. This will remind me how much you love me. This will be my private show, from my private actress, my Katherina." He'd looked at me like there would actually be a possibility of me saying anything but yes. "My adorable Katie, you *do* love me, don't you?" Then he'd poured me another glass and I'd gulped it down and felt terrific. It was the same feeling like when I was on stage. Which I was, in a way, I guess. The liqueur, the way he looked at me, the flowers, the gift. God. I felt all warm and giddy and bold, powerful in a Katherina sort of way. I even gifted Evan with parts of Katherina's submission speech. That was still pretty early on in the night, so I got most of it right. I think.

"Katie?" He was so, so gorgeous. "Katie, will you do this for me?"

Why are our bodies soft, and weak, and smooth,
Unapt to toil and trouble in the world,
But that our soft conditions and our hearts
Should well agree with our external parts?
. . . And place your hands below your husband's foot.
In token of which duty, if he please,
My hand is ready, may it do him ease.

And he laughed! I loved when I could make him laugh. Apparently I didn't even need the stage, just Shakespeare's words were enough. He pulled me to him and growled his Petruchio response.

Why, there's a wench! Come on, and kiss me, Kate.

And my heart soared when he said it.

The flowers stared at me accusingly. I picked up the vase, held my breath and ran out into the hall all the way to the garbage chute. I opened the little door and threw the whole thing down the chute—water, flowers, vase and all. I exhaled.

"*Kiss me.*"

Dear God.

I felt my way back to the apartment. When he called, I was going to ask him: how could anyone who loved anyone make someone do the things he'd made me do?

Had he *made* me do them? Had he? That was the worst part, I wasn't sure. I barely made it back in time to puke in the kitchen sink.

"Don't you like the phone? I even programmed your little friend Lisa in there, and Travis, too." Evan had looked so sweet, so loving then, so like a little boy. "I know I've been hogging you." He looked at the floor. "This way, you'll be able to at least talk to them on your down time." He kissed my eyes.

He laughed, I giggled. He loved me. I loved him. Of course I loved him. How could I *not* love him? "I love you more than anyone, more than Kate loves Petruchio." But he didn't believe me. And I had to prove it. I caught an image. Evan grabbed me as I moved, and pulled me onto the floor. I was afraid, but for just a second. Last night or now? My head spun dangerously.

No, not afraid. I was angry, and I had every right to be. I was drunk, and Evan pushed and pushed, and I wasn't ready and still he pushed. Right, not afraid, I was furious, and when he called, I would give him what for. I was going to tell him that he'd had no right, I was out of my head drunk, and, and, dear God, whole parts of the night felt good. But I wasn't going to tell him that. I couldn't even acknowledge that to myself without rushing for the toilet.

Shame washed over me again. Finally, I was what my mother had been accusing me of being all these years.

The bottle! I got up from the sofa carefully and began to search for the evidence. I was for sure afraid of my mother, and if she found that bottle, my life would be over. I overturned cushions and opened every cupboard door before I had to stop for another throw-up. What came out was clearer now, more like spit than barf. I scrubbed up again. My hands were raw from all that Ajax.

He must have taken the bottle with him. I'd ask when he called.

I'd have to make sure to wear long sleeves and high collars until everything faded.

My head was clearing a bit, and by dinnertime I could hold down water. Joey and Mom would be home soon. Evan had better call before they got back, or I'd have to go to my room and close the door while I tore into him. But he was so beautiful, and he said *I* was beautiful. And I almost believed him. I could not stop looking at him, all fair and cut like a statue, yet sometimes so sweet and unsure. And he said he loved me, he really did, and I'd make him say it when he called.

. He had worn a blindingly white shirt in the thinnest, softest possible cotton. "Like it? I bought it just for you, I wanted to look nice for you tonight, Katie." Then he'd opened the bottle.

I inhaled and memorized the scent of him, imprinted Evan on me. Did he know that, could he tell? He always smelled like what I imagined a beach would smell like—sun, waves, wind, clean and strong. I had another flash and braced myself for a slow, rolling wave of shame.

I glanced at my bedside clock: 5:57 p.m. Maybe I wouldn't even answer the phone. That'd teach him. No, I'd answer it and take him apart.

My stomach began churning at 6:18. It was different from the hangover nausea. This was fear, pure and simple, no ribbons and pearls on this one. I started pacing. This was not the terror of the flashbacks, or the shame of broiling anger, this was fear of the biggest, baddest kind.

Dear God in heaven, what if he didn't call?

Chapter Twenty~Seven

"That was really, uh, how shall I put this . . . NOT VERY GOOD!" Travis yelled. "What is with you two this morning?"

I looked over at Katie. She looked down at the floor. She'd hardly been able to make eye contact with me during the whole rehearsal. That was good. If she'd been able to meet my eye I would have had difficulty meeting hers.

"It's Monday morning . . . early Monday morning," I mumbled.

"I know that you're not happy about practices being two a day now," Travis said. "I know no one is, but we're coming down to the short strokes and we have to do it right . . . a lot righter than this has been going this morning. Okay, once more, from the same place, line 23 . . . Katie . . . you have the first line," Travis called out. "And please, with a little feeling, a little emotion, and some *connection*. Now go."

Katie took a deep breath and I knew she was getting into character once again.

"*Husband, let's follow to see the end of this ado,*" Katie said.

"*First kiss me, Kate, and we will,*" I replied.

"*What, in the midst of the street?*" she demanded.

"*What, are thou . . . thou . . . ashamed of me?*" The word stuck in my mouth. I *did* feel ashamed.

She hesitated. I was positive she knew the next line. She must have been thinking the same thing I was.

"*No sir, God forbid, but ashamed to kiss,*" she said.

"*Why then, let's home again. Come sirrah, let's away.*"

"*Nay, I will give thee a kiss.*"

Katie looked up at me—practically for the first time all morning. This was where she was supposed to lean forward and we were to kiss. Neither of us moved.

"Come on!" Travis yelled. "It's not like the two of you haven't kissed before!" I heard giggling from the peanut gallery.

We both leaned in and gave each other a little peck.

"You're not kissing your mother up there!" Travis yelled. "I've had more passionate kisses from some of my aunts . . . and I'm still scarred for life! How about if we all take a break so you can rethink this and I can scrub my mind clear of those images of Aunt Sophie. Everybody back in five!"

I reached out and took Katie's hand. "We need to talk."

I led her off stage. She didn't resist. She came along willingly. I looked out and caught Lisa looking at me—there was real anger in her eyes. Had Katie told her what had happened? No, that look didn't mean anything—she already hated me.

There were people backstage. There were people everywhere.

"I don't want an audience," I said.

I pushed open the stage door and we headed outside. The door closed behind us and we were alone. Now I just had to figure out what to say.

"Are you okay?" I asked.

"Just a little confused . . . you didn't call."

"*You* didn't call either. I thought you wouldn't want to speak to *me*," I said.

I'd spent the day sweating whether there was going to be a knock on the door—the police asking me questions about what had happened—that she'd woken up and thought about the whole thing. I guess I should have been there when she woke up but I just couldn't face her.

"I feel so bad about what happened . . . can you ever forgive me?" I asked.

"Forgive you?"

"I got you drunk."

"We both had too much to drink," she said.

"But I brought the alcohol, I poured the drinks, it was my idea."

"You didn't force me to drink." She paused. "I just thought you wouldn't want to see me . . . after we . . ." She let the sentence trail off.

"How could you even think that?" I asked. "You were drunk and I took advantage of you."

"I wasn't *that* drunk. You didn't force me to do anything."

"Are you sure?"

"Completely," she said, unconvincingly. She looked up at me and tried to smile but didn't quite get there.

I held up my phone. "And I wanted to talk to you about the pictures I took."

She nodded her head. "I wanted to talk to you about them too."

"You know I'd never show anybody."

"I know that. But . . . I don't know . . . it's just . . ."

"That they make you feel uncomfortable," I said. "I knew that when I was taking them, and I know that now. I had too much to drink too. I never would have done that if *I* wasn't drunk." I almost believed myself. "But you don't have to worry. They're gone. I erased them. You can check if you want."

"I don't have to check." She smiled. "I believe you. Besides, I don't even know how to check."

"It's right here," I said. I pressed two buttons—the second to show the image. "This is the only picture I kept."

I showed Katie the first shot I'd taken that night, the one when she was still dressed. It was nice. She was pretty . . . no, not pretty, she was beautiful. It almost surprised me. I'd been looking through the pictures all weekend and now, boom, there it was. She was *so* beautiful.

"Could I use it as the wallpaper on my phone?" I asked.

"Of course!"

"Then, is all forgiven?"

"There's nothing to forgive," she replied. "When you didn't call I just thought that after what happened, and after you saw where I live, that—"

"That I wouldn't want to call you?" I asked.

She nodded her head.

"Now you should be apologizing to me if you think I'm that shallow," I said.

"I don't! Honestly! It's just that, you know, compared to where you live."

"Where I live doesn't matter, just like it doesn't matter where you live. What matters is who you are. Speaking of which, when are you going to introduce me to your mother?"

"Never!"

"Are you ashamed of me, like in the play?" I asked.

She laughed. "I'm proud to be your girl. It's just that you don't know my mother."

"And I won't until I meet her."

"That's not what I mean. You have to understand, she isn't like your parents. They're so nice and supportive."

"You don't know my father!" I blurted out before I could stop myself. "He's a lot of things but I wouldn't include *nice* or *supportive* on that list."

"But he seems so . . ."

"*Seems* and *are* are so different. He's . . . he's . . . I don't know how to explain it exactly. It's just that you're an innocent," I replied. "People can fool you."

That may have been the most honest thing I'd ever said to her. She looked bewildered.

"And your innocence is one of the things I love about you." I pulled her close and kissed her and she kissed back—long and deep and passionate.

"Hey!"

We stopped and looked over. Travis was standing at the stage door, peering out.

"That's the sort of kiss I was looking for. Now you two should either get back up on stage or get a room! And I think I'd prefer the former!"

"You go ahead," I said to Katie. "I'll be there in just a minute."

She hesitated. "Go." I gave her a gentle push. "I'll be there in just a minute."

Travis held the door for her and the two of them hesitated, looking back at me.

"I'll be right there!" I yelled out. "I'm not running away from home. I just want to gather my thoughts."

They disappeared inside. I pulled out my phone and tapped the app for tape recorder and then pushed play. Katie's voice came out.

"*I wasn't that drunk. You didn't force me to do anything.*"

"*Are you sure?*"

"*Completely.*"

I now had her saying it. Just like I still had those pictures of her on my laptop at home. I had two types of proof, but even more important, I had control of the situation, control of her.

You're in charge, you're in control, a voice in my head said. But it wasn't my voice. It was my father's.

Chapter Twenty-Eight

.♡.

He still loved me, and nothing else mattered. Really. In fact, Evan had said he loved me more than ever because I had proved *my love* for him by trusting him and everything. Of course I trusted Evan. I *loved* Evan.

And that's what I told Lisa when she interrogated me in the dressing room. She kind of barged in unexpectedly after Wednesday afternoon's dress rehearsal and caught me changing. She saw.

"What the . . . is he . . . ?"

"It's okay." I put my hand up as if it were a singular force field that would block out her words. It worked. Lisa shut her mouth. And then opened it again.

"Katie?!"

"It's not what you think," I said, buttoning up my blouse as fast as I could. The marks that she could see were mainly on my arms. They were purple and angry-looking, and while they looked worse than they had a few days ago they didn't hurt. Any more.

"What I think? What *I* think! You have no idea what I think." She walked all around me. "Travis said he thought there was something hinky going on between the two of you at Monday morning's rehearsal. Katie . . ."

"Evan simply doesn't know his own strength when he's

gripped in the throes of passion. Of course, *you* wouldn't know about that."

I don't know why I added that snotty little tag, or why I was talking to her all snotty-like to begin with. Lisa looked genuinely sad and scared for me. Maybe that was it. Yeah. How dare she? I didn't want or need her pity party. I'd never seen this side of her before. She seemed to think that she was some kind of all-seeing, all-knowing Buddha.

"Oh my God, Katie. You didn't, did you? You did, didn't you? Did you?" She sort of fell back into the basin we were using as a makeshift makeup table. "Not with a guy like . . ." She ate the rest of that sentence, which was just as well.

I was having real trouble buttoning up anything and I couldn't remember where my jeans were. The cold of the granite floor shot up my legs and shocked my heart. I tried to read her expression. Was Lisa angry at me, or just surprised that a boy like Evan would even want me?

"And for your personal info," Lisa said, "I'll have you know that I have made love before, Katie, with two lovely young men and one complete jerk, *none* of whom left marks on me. Grip of passion? He has a grip on you, all right."

Three guys? I did the math. When? What was that about? The jerk? What about the jerk—did he force her, make her do things she didn't want to do? It would explain so much. A *friend* would know about that. A friend would have shared that with me before she was using it as some lame excuse to lecture me. When the shock wore off, I resumed my righteous pose.

"Evan got completely and totally lost in how much he loves me, and that's okay because I love him, too." At last, I located my socks. "Evan Campbell is my everything, and if you cared at all, Lisa, you would be thrilled for me. Unlike your *three* guys, he is the real deal for me."

I didn't look at her after that little soliloquy, which was hard, it was really tight in there. I thought she'd tear me limb from limb, or leave slamming the door. Instead, Lisa just sat down and nodded.

I gave up on the complexity of buttonholes and concentrated my shaking hands on socks. Just then the door swung open and Travis came in butt first because his arms were loaded down with three grande frappuccinos.

"Hey, girlfriends, I'm here for coffee intervention!"

"Travis!" I yelled. "Travis, I'm practically naked here!"

He looked me over from top to bottom. "Honey, I hate to crush you, but the sight of your floral panties doesn't do a thing for me." He tilted his head. "I think I'd like more action in the chest area."

"That's just rude, and that's not the point!" I stomped around in my socks and buttoned blouse. I was still searching for my pants when Lisa threw them at me.

"What did I miss?" Travis asked.

"She and Evan are doing it," Lisa said.

"Just once . . . it's not the same thing." But then I held my breath both so that I could successfully zip up my new jeans . . . and because I was afraid she'd tell him about the marks.

Why was I afraid?

"Well, it was only a matter of time. It was inevitable," Travis said. "And if you didn't I might have."

"Travis!" We both groaned.

"Well, sure, he's a bit intense, but he's pretty darned pretty . . ."

Lisa tossed someone's orphaned sock at him.

I grabbed my drink and sat down on the cold granite bench,

semi-naked, and it didn't matter. I was with my friends and they were razzing me. This felt right. I was safe and I was loved. Okay, if not loved, at least liked a lot.

"Thanks for the frappuccino, Mr. Director."

"Anything for my leading lady." He squinted at me. "You need more of them. Are you losing weight?"

"Well, Evan is used to dating very fashionably slim—"

"Anorexics. Lollipops, all head no body!" snorted Lisa. "Remember, I know the schools he went to, I know the type."

"You keep your meat on you, girl," said Travis. "He's not dating them, he fell in love with you, with my leading lady, my actress, my future movie star!"

My face burned. I flashed to Evan taking pictures. I gulped down a shot of shame with the frappuccino.

"Hey." Travis looked at me quizzically. "He buys you stuff nonstop, takes you everywhere, can't keep his hands off you and is devoted to you. You've got that boy wrapped around your little finger."

Travis kept teasing me about who was "taming" who. Lisa was quiet, but Travis really liked that one. He said I was executing an inversion of the play.

Like I could ever tame Evan.

As we left, Lisa whispered in my ear, "I'm here, Katie. Always. Don't forget it. Even Travis is here, on your side . . ." We watched him sing, sway and sashay down the hall to some almost-big Emo hit. "Yup," she continued, "whether you want him or not, Travis is here for you too. Got it?"

"Jeez, are you blind or jealous or what, Lisa? Love is love, and love is always a good thing!"

"Got it?" Lisa repeated. She blocked the doorway.

"Okay, got it already!" I threw my arm around her and pushed us both through the door.

This friend thing had so many sides and complications to it. If only Evan could have seen. how wonderful both Travis and Lisa were. If he had understood that they were my only friends, and how they had got me through the days before he came ... then I bet that he'd have changed his mind about them in a heartbeat. And I'd try to explain that to him.

"They're losers, and they'll drag you down with them," Evan said. "Katie, you don't see it, because you're so sweet and naive. But I'm telling you, they're the bottom of the social barrel. Okay, Travis is a pretty good director, and maybe one day he'll make something of himself that way, but it's a long shot." He shrugged. "But Lisa?" He kissed my eyes. "First off, I think she's queer too." He caught my look and mistook it. "Which is a who cares and everything, but she's just a social zero on top of that. It doesn't matter that she comes from money. She's blown her social cred at every school she's been at."

"No, see, it's just that she doesn't care about—"

Evan pulled me up off his sofa, where we'd spent the last two hours running lines. "After the play, maybe over the holidays, I'm going to introduce you to some of my old friends. You'll see the difference, baby."

I shivered in anticipation. There was so much there in that one little. sentence. First, that he talked about the holidays and that we'd still be together then. Second, that he couldn't wait to introduce me to all his friends. In one and a half seconds I had visions of us at someone's ski chalet. There we were on the designer rustic-like sofa and on the floor, laughing with all the other beautiful blond couples having rum toddies in front of a fireplace and talking about the merits of Princeton over Yale. Evan would proudly point out how I was the creative one, destined for greatness because of my theatre school scholarship.

It dawned on me that that was the very first time I had ever stitched a little dream for myself about the future. But now— because, with Evan, anything was possible—now I could dream. My mother would beg forgiveness as I packed for my big weekend away. I'd forgive her for whatever it was because I wouldn't want the thing hanging over my head as I took skiing lessons. I'd have to buy ski chalet–type sweaters and clear lip gloss. I would love his sophisticated friends and, after an initial slightly shy nervousness on my part, they would love me and find those traits endearing and genuine. I began to understand how Travis and Lisa would not fit into that Ralph Lauren ad. I also decided it wasn't worth the effort correcting him about Lisa. It didn't matter, and anyway, maybe he was right.

"Now, how about we do a little something to help us relax?"

I stiffened and he gripped just a little tighter.

"Evan, your parents . . ."

"Chill, baby." He glanced at his watch. "Mom is away at something and Dad is in his study, thinking about how to make everyone around him pay."

"Evan!"

"It's true, baby. It's time you grew up a bit. I keep trying to tell you about . . . about him. You can't always believe what you see."

He gripped tighter still. I winced. His fingers shifted and were probably covering old bruises.

"Don't you want to make me happy, Katie, my Kate?"

I nodded.

"Take off your top." He took a step back. "Don't look like that, Kate! How about a little enthusiasm? You know I'd do anything for *you*."

I lifted my pullover.

"Now . . ."

My stomach clenched. I heard his father's footsteps in the study above us.

"Good girl," Evan whispered. "And if you continue to be a good girl, we'll go to Josh's party tomorrow night."

"Really, Evan?" I jumped into his arms. He had point-blank refused to even consider it until now. Josh was throwing a party for both the cast and some of his basketball buddies in a "two worlds collide" kind of theme. It sounded like the most exciting and glamorous thing in the world to me. Apparently, it sounded lame to Evan.

"Promise?" I asked.

Evan nodded. Just barely, but he did.

"Now . . ." he said.

Chapter Twenty-Nine

⋅♡⋅

Finally Friday came, the party was that night. There was no afternoon rehearsal. Travis said he didn't want to burn us out. I think he was just dead tired. He was always making notes, talking to himself in the halls and compulsively blocking out the stage for scenery and our set pieces. The play was bleeding him dry. It was hard to tell if Travis was pale under all that white makeup, but the boy was pooped. He said he wasn't even going to go to the party.

"Bull," said Lisa when I told her in algebra. "I bet he has a fantasy about turning a point guard, and he's never going to get a better chance than at Josh's 'Colliding Worlds.'"

I wore a fire-engine-red boat-neck cashmere sweater that Evan had bought for me, with a terrific and tasteful black miniskirt that I'd scored from the Old Navy sales bin—some habits die hard, I guess. I'd also bought a pair of heart-stoppingly gorgeous black, floral-patterned stockings that had cost more than I could have wrapped my imagination around even two months before. But I loved, loved, *loved* them and how they made my legs look. I promised myself that I would always wash them by hand in the sink and dry them on the shower rod. My exquisite $32.50 stockings would never, ever see the inside of a washer or dryer. I would wear them on my graduation from theatre school. I only hoped that I would feel and look half as good then as I did that night.

"Well, well!" Joey whistled.

My heart stopped for a second before I smiled. It was just Joey.

"You look like big bucks, kid."

That was high praise indeed, and I beamed at him. Right before I stepped out into the hall, I heard Mom call out, "Yeah, you look real nice, sweetie. Have a good time."

That would have been a great motherly touch, except I knew she'd said that for Joey's benefit, not for mine.

"Remember, you still got your bakery shift," she yelled after me.

I had never felt prettier in my entire life. "Note the date and time," I giggled in an empty elevator, "8:07, November 27!"

I couldn't stop looking at my legs. I, Katie Rosario, was pretty, and I was going to meet my fabulous boyfriend and go to my first A-List party—well, pretty much my first party, period. I took my terrific legs straight to Evan's waiting Audi. He growled like a tiger when he saw me. And my heart purred in response.

Josh lived in Forest Heights, not Evan's snack bracket, but pretty posh all the same. I would have to remember the address for Joey: 4082 Poplar Lane. We didn't even get to the door before it swung wide open and we were greeted by an exuberantly loaded and freshly "unwired" Josh.

"Here she is, finally! Kate, my darling shrew! The only thing I miss about the whole torturous play is holding you, gorgeous!" And with that Josh smothered me in a monster hug and then dragged me into the party.

"Damn, woman, I swear you get better-looking every time I see you!" Josh waved his arm around and a scattered group of actors and jocks looked over at us. Lisa and Travis were with Danny, grinning at me from the sound system. Brittney had her arms wrapped around Danny. He was smiling like he was six years old and waiting to unwrap his presents on Christmas morning.

"Hey, everybody!" Josh raised a Corona. "Our star is here! *Now* we can party!"

And everybody cheered, everybody looked, everybody *saw* me. The only thing I worried about was how to hang on to that feeling. It was a miracle. How could it be anything but the best night of my life?

Chapter Thirty

I unballed my fists so I could dig the car keys out of my pocket. I clicked the remote so the doors unlocked and quickly climbed into the car. All I wanted was to get away from there—and away from *her*. But I was only going to be able to do *one* of those things because *she* sat down in the passenger seat beside me. I gunned the engine, laying a patch and spraying up gravel that pinged noisily against the car at the curb behind me.

Katie glanced back over her shoulder and looked like she was going to say something, but she didn't. That was the first smart decision she'd made all night. I turned the corner and the tires squealed. I didn't have time to slow down. I just wanted to get her home and get away before I said anything or did anything that I might—

"Are you angry about something?" Katie asked.

"What makes you think I'm angry?" I questioned through clenched teeth.

"It's just that . . . that . . . you're not talking."

"Maybe it's good that at least one of us is smart enough to keep their mouth shut," I snapped—although by saying that I obviously wasn't following my own advice.

"What do you mean?" I could hear the surprise and concern in her voice.

I didn't answer. I'd just try harder to keep quiet, to stay in control, at least of myself.

"Is it something I said?" she asked.

"Said and did," I snapped. So much for keeping my mouth closed.

"What did I do? What did I say? What?"

"I'm not blind and I'm not an idiot!"

"But . . . but . . . but–"

"You think I couldn't see how you were acting around those guys?" I demanded. "You think I didn't notice?"

"Didn't notice what?" There was a tinge of desperation in her voice.

"I saw you flirting with them!" I snapped. "I saw you throw yourself at Josh."

"I didn't! I wasn't anything with Josh!"

"Just the others?" I demanded.

"I wasn't flirting with anybody!"

I laughed. "I saw the way you were acting. I heard what you were saying."

"I was just talking to people at the party. I wasn't flirting with anybody . . . honestly! What did I say?"

"I'm not going to repeat it. And it wasn't just the words, it was the way you were acting! I wasn't born yesterday. I saw the signs, the way you tilted your head, laughing at what they said even when it wasn't funny, pushed out your chest, practically draping yourself over Josh!"

She didn't answer, which was an admission of guilt. I took another turn quickly and the car practically tilted onto two wheels. Out of the corner of my eye I saw her gripping the seat with both hands.

"I wasn't throwing myself at anybody!" Her voice was shaky. "Honestly, I would never do that to you, never!"

"There you go again, thinking that I'm an idiot and I don't know what I saw."

"No, you're the smartest person I've ever met!"

"Smart enough to know when somebody is flirting, practically throwing herself at somebody, and doing it right in front of my eyes! How do you think that makes me feel?"

"I'm sorry . . . I didn't know . . . I mean, I wasn't trying to flirt . . . if I was I'm sorry . . . so sorry!"

"Sorry you were flirting or sorry you got caught?"

"Sorry for everything. I didn't mean to flirt with anybody . . . I would never do that! I've never been to a party before. You have to believe me, please, you have to believe me!"

She reached over to take my arm and I brushed her hand away.

"I wasn't doing anything," she said again. I could tell she was close to tears. Lots of females could fake tears—big deal. "I wasn't flirting with anybody . . . I was just trying to be friendly."

"Is that what you call it?" I demanded. "Being *friendly*? In my world we have another word for a girl who throws herself at a guy like that, and the word isn't *friendly*."

"What are you saying?" she gasped.

"Are you telling me that you've never been with anybody except me?"

"I . . . you know that . . . I . . . don't know what to say," she sputtered.

"How many others? How many, Katie?"

She didn't say anything.

"It's probably better you don't say anything than lie to me! I know when you're lying. And from what you didn't say I know the answer. How many have there been? So many that it's taking you too long to count them all?"

She started crying. I felt a pull in my heart and then hardened it. I wasn't going to be manipulated by her turning on the waterworks.

I pushed the car a little harder. We were passing other cars like they were practically standing still.

"You're scaring me," she sobbed. "Please, could you slow down . . . please?"

"You want me to slow down?" I asked in amazement.

"Please," she said. "I'm feeling–"

I slammed on the brakes, squealed over to the side, cutting off a car that honked at me, and then pulled off to the shoulder and brought the car to a sudden stop.

I glared at her–she looked terrified.

"Get out," I said.

"What?"

"Get out of the car."

"You want me to . . . to get out?"

"Yeah, right now. Get out of my car!" I yelled.

"But, but . . ."

I unsnapped her seatbelt and then reached overtop of her to open the door.

"Get out! Now!" I screamed.

She hesitated, and I pushed her. She stumbled out, tripping and falling before regaining her feet, a stunned look on her face, staring back into the open door, back at me.

The tears practically exploded out of her. For a split second I felt sorry, sad for me, sorry that I'd just done what I'd done. And then I remembered what she'd done to *me*.

"But how will I get home?" she cried.

"You can walk home . . . or maybe walk back to the party and one of those guys can drive you home . . . or to wherever you want to go!"

"I'm sorry . . . I'm so sorry!" she cried.

"Too late!"

I reached over and grabbed the door, slamming it shut. I threw the car into drive and hit the gas pedal, racing away, leaving her standing on the side of the road. I caught a glance of her in my rear-view mirror before the darkness swallowed her up. A few drops of rain fell on the windshield, and then I saw Katie's shoes on the floor of the car. She was alone on the side of the road, in stocking feet, in the rain, in the dark.

And she deserved it.

Chapter Thirty-One

❤

"Stupid! I am so, so stupid!"

I said that out loud to the soupy darkness as I watched Evan drive away. I didn't move for at least ten minutes. I was rooted to the curb, barely breathing, waiting for him to turn around, to come back for me. My shoes—which I'd kicked off when I got in—and my purse were still in the car.

Finally, I got up and picked my way over to a street lamp on the corner of Walnut and Chester Ave. Now I could see that my beautiful stockings were ruined. And there was a messy gash at the side of my left knee from when he'd pushed me out of the car. Was that blood?

He wasn't coming back. I had stopped crying the moment he drove away. I was too stunned to cry.

Stunned and stupid, so stupid I didn't even know what I'd done wrong. Flirting? When? How? I wasn't sure I even knew *how* to flirt. I mean, I knew when I saw it on TV or in the movies, but to actually, actively *flirt*? It would have taken more guts than I had. But did I, was I? If Evan said I was, I must have . . . and then it started to rain harder . . . less than a downpour, more than a drizzle, enough to get good and wet.

He really wasn't coming back.

Okay, then.

I angled my watch under the light: 1:35 a.m. I could still get home and make my shift. If I could figure out how to get to there from here. If I could move.

"Come on now, Katie. One foot in front of the other." My knee stung as the ripped stocking pattern bit into the drying blood. "Okay, okay, Chestnut should take me to that long street that also has a tree name, the one we turned onto just before Queen Street. Then if I stick to Queen the whole way, I should get home." It was the super-long route, but one that would be guaranteed to work. I thought.

How *could* he?

I started walking. It hurt less when I walked, so I kept going. The sidewalk was smoother than I'd have thought on my almost-bare feet, maybe because it was slicked with drizzle. It was a surprising kind of thing. Oh sure, I'd step on a pebble here or there, or on lost clumps of oak leaves huddled together for warmth, but overall the sidewalk was very smooth and very, very cold. Each step pierced me with a shot of shivering. It would be the cold that stopped me.

Flirting? I absolutely for sure had not been flirting. I'd just been so happy to be there with Evan, looking pretty. I hadn't even danced with Josh, no matter how many times he asked, and he asked a lot, or even with Danny, just with Travis and Lisa. And just for that one dance at midnight. The three of us had never been at a party together, let alone one like that. We couldn't get over ourselves, and we certainly didn't need anything extra to feel higher than we already did. But I *must* have been flirting. I was so bad at seeing and sorting these things out. Stupid.

It was like with Nick Kormos all over again. I should have known about him. Shouldn't have done whatever I must have been doing. Should have seen it coming. Should have, but didn't.

Mr. Kormos was very handsome, with that heroic *you're in safe hands now* handsomeness that all TV doctors have. Mom lived for his every breath, and maybe I did too, a little. No one had even pretended to want to be my father before. For my twelfth birthday Nick Kormos had bought me a pair of pink Ugg boots, $168.29. I knew the price because he showed me the bill. I still had them. And the bill. A week later he touched me.

"She won't believe you." That's what Nick Kormos said that first time. "So don't bother running to Mommy." He gulped down the rest of his Chivas. "I'll say you were asking for it. I'll say you were *begging* for it."

Begging for it? Begging for what? That? Like I said, stupid.

Mr. Kormos was right and I knew it, so I didn't say anything after that first time, or the second. I didn't know what to say exactly. It was wrong and bad, but so was I. Or it wouldn't have happened.

And we were both right. My mother did not believe me, even when she walked in with him on top of me while I was fighting with everything I had. And she blamed me. Just like he'd said. They were the adults. So it must have been my fault. And . . . I must have been flirting at the party.

A symphony of construction noises in my head joined a chorus of shame just as I was coming up to Queen. I was tired of lugging around all that noise, and all those pictures in my head. I was tired, period. There was still such a long way to go.

A car approached from the opposite side of the street, its lights tunnelling through the ink of the night. The lights were bluish—Audi lights, Evan's lights. The car slowed. Evan? He'd come back for me. He pulled up across the street. The window slid down and a smile slid up. Not Evan. It was a man in his thirties.

"Hi, honey, need a lift?"

Chapter Thirty-Two

I pushed the button to roll down the passenger-side window. Rain fell into the car, but I needed it open so I could see better. My father would have something to say about me ruining the leather if he noticed it—who was I kidding, he noticed everything.

But between the rain on the windshield and the darkness it was hard to see, and I had to have the window open so I could scan the side of the road . . . I should have seen her by now. Where *had* she gotten to? I hadn't been gone for more than fifteen or twenty minutes. That was how long it had taken for my blood to stop boiling and for my brain to take over. I'd spun the car around and raced back to look for her, to where I thought she could have walked to. But she wasn't there. She wasn't anywhere. Had she walked back to the party, or had she just made a phone call, maybe to Josh or somebody else, and they'd come and picked her up? If that was what had happened there'd be a price to pay, for him and for her and . . . Stop, just stop.

Calm down. I should have been *hoping* that someone else had come to her rescue, because if not, a whole lot of worse things could have happened. It was dark, and the streets were deserted.

What if somebody had been driving along and saw her on the side of the road and pulled over and picked her up? Even she wouldn't be naive or stupid enough to get in the car with a stranger . . . even if it was raining and she had no shoes. Would she? I looked over at her shoes. She loved those black shoes. If I'd known, I never would have driven away with her shoes, but by the time I noticed them it was too late to turn back. Too late to not act like a total douche bag.

She had to be smart enough not to get into the car with a stranger. Unless somebody forced her. There were all sorts of twisted people in the world. My father had told me, time and time again, that you could never really trust anybody, that people could be kind to your face but turn away for a second and they'd slip a knife in your back. I'd seen enough to know that he was right—at least about that. People weren't to be trusted . . . but Katie wasn't like people. I *did* trust her. I never should have said those things. I never should have made her get out of the car. I never should have driven away.

If only I could find her and we could talk and . . . wait a second. The phone. I could call and ask where she was.

I pushed the speed dial I'd programmed for her. "Come on, come on, start ringing."

Her phone did start ringing—from the floor in front of the passenger seat. And as it rang I saw in the light that it was beside her purse. Bad enough that she didn't have shoes, but she didn't have her phone or her purse either. Her phone kept ringing—that stupid Eminem song, "Not Afraid." We'd argued about it. I hated that song, it was crude and the opposite of everything I knew about Katie—even if she didn't know it herself. I threw my phone onto the floor. *Katie, where are you?*

What if something had happened to her? Lots of people had seen us leave together, and some had probably seen us drive away, and anybody with half a brain would have noticed that I was mad at her. If something happened to her, they'd all blame me, maybe even think that I did it. And if anybody investigated, the truth about my past would come out and then they'd think I did it for sure.

Of course, if something bad happened to her it really *was* my fault. I was the one who'd made her leave the car. I was the one who'd pushed my girl, my Katie, out the door and into the night. If something happened to her, they wouldn't need to blame me because I was already blaming myself.

There was somebody up ahead at the side of the road! I slowed down and—it was just a man out walking his dog. I thought about stopping and asking him if he'd seen her, but there was no point. If he'd seen her, then I would have seen her too. There was only one thing to do. I had to get to her apartment and wait.

Chapter Thirty-Three

The man flashed a nice smile that reminded me of . . .

"You're getting soaked. Let me at least drop you off at the subway station."

I inhaled sharply.

"Look, you can sit in the back if you're nervous."

That was nice of him. I started to cross the street. Nervous? Wait.

"Honey, you're going to catch pneumonia out there. You don't have to tell me your story but at least get out of the rain."

He reminded me of someone. A dad or—

"Come on, let me take you home."

Nick? He reminded me of Nick Kormos. Could it be?

"Mr. Kormos, Nick?" I called out.

"Yeah, sure." He smiled again. "I can be Mr. Kormos, if you want. Just get in, sweetie."

With a ride I'd be home in ten minutes. I couldn't walk home barefoot, that was nuts. I started to cross the street.

"That's it, baby, you get in and Nick Kormos will take care of you."

I was back on the sidewalk before either of us knew it. "What the . . . ? Hey, kid!"

I'd be on Queen in a couple of blocks with the bright retail store signage. Streetcars would go by, and surely even some people. I'd be safe on Queen.

"No thanks, sir."

"Sir!?" The word seemed to make him angry.

"I live just around the corner. Thanks for the offer, but I've had enough Nick Kormoses in my life." And with that, I hobbled off with as much dignity as I could muster in torn stockings, bare feet and a fake down Value Village ski jacket.

I heard him curse as he sped away, like a snake slithering into a hole in the night. I glanced back over my shoulder.

"Good girl, Katie," I said out loud again. "Maybe you're not so stupid after all."

Chapter Thirty-Four

I pushed the buzzer for her apartment again, for the tenth time. I wasn't sure what the point was. Either she still wasn't home, or she was home and wasn't answering the buzzer. I was pretty sure her mother was away again or she wouldn't have been able to stay so late at the party. For all I knew, Katie was sitting up in her apartment looking down at me on the lobby's closed-circuit camera. Did that camera even work? If they could afford a camera, you would have thought they could have paid to get the smell out of the entranceway.

I looked back up at the camera in case she was looking down at me. I didn't care if she didn't want to talk to me, and I certainly didn't expect her to let me up. All I wanted was to know that she was all right, that she was up there, that she was safe.

If it had been me up there, I wouldn't have answered either. Not just because I wouldn't have known what to say, but to punish the person who had left me in the rain, to keep him spinning in the wind. I'd never been left on the side of the road in the rain, but I knew what it was like to be humiliated, and abandoned. Made to feel like I wasn't good enough, never good enough. That was how they made me feel in the end.

I slumped down to the floor and covered my face with my hands. If I'd believed there was a God who listened and answered prayers, I would have said one right there.

"I just want her to be okay," I said, my words just a whisper, a plea . . . maybe it *was* a prayer. That was how desperate I felt. If it was, it would have been the first prayer of mine that had been answered.

Chapter Thirty-Five

The rain stopped the instant I rounded onto Queen Street. There was more traffic and the odd fellow traveller. Safe.

Evan had asked if there had been anyone else. "How many others? How many, Katie?" Did Nick Kormos count? Maybe he did, and Evan had sensed it somehow. Maybe guys just knew these things. I had made him so angry. He must have known. Somehow he must have known that I was dirty and now he was punishing me.

I was exhausted and giddy with the cold by then. Evan thoughts chased each other around and around in me, in ever-tighter circles. I was talking out loud to myself by this point. If anyone noticed as I passed them by, they sure didn't let on. We were an interesting species, we shoeless, homeless or just plain stoned people of the night. We were also pretty much a "live and let live" kind of folk.

By the time I got to Muldar and Queen I decided that Evan wasn't punishing me. Maybe he was pulling a Petruchio.

Petruchio *breaks* Katherina, after all, and in a totally humiliating way. He *tames* her. In fact, in Act IV, scene 3—the one Evan and I had the most trouble with—Petruchio pretty much bullies, starves and manipulates her until Kate finally submits. She even stops arguing and comes around to agreeing with him that the sun is actually the moon.

Petruchio: I say it is the moon.

Katherina: I know it is the moon.

Petruchio: Nay, then you lie. It is the blessed sun.

Katherina: Then, God be blessed, it is the blessed sun.

Wow, there I was on Queen Street in the middle of the night, cold, shoeless and quoting Shakespeare out loud. Just me, the drunks, the crazies, the homeless and Bill.

My mind went back to that scene. Petruchio treats her so badly it's breathtaking. By the end of Act V, scene 1, he's making Kate kiss him in public to show the world that she is not ashamed of him. The thing is, in the name of love, Petruchio successfully torments Katherina into being a lover and a better human. Maybe Evan was trying to tame me or test me or . . . something. He was so angry. I must have hurt him so badly, flirting like that. I should have known what I was doing.

I got to my block just before 3:30 a.m. Thank God at least I had my key in my ski jacket pocket, my key and my lip chap. I wished I had remembered about that a little earlier.

I walked into the lobby, and I was so eager to get in and up to my apartment that I almost fell on top of him.

"Evan! Evan, what are you . . . ?"

Chapter Thirty-Six

I felt so embarrassed being caught sitting on the floor, my head in my hands. It was humiliating. But then I saw her, really saw her, as I struggled to my feet. Katie was soaked to the bone, her hair and clothing plastered to her body, her stockings—those beautiful stockings she was so proud of—ripped and torn, the feet worn through and a rip down the side of one of them . . . I saw blood. Oh my God.

"I am so sorry," I whispered.

She looked so sad, so stunned. Even through the wet of the rain I could see the tears she'd been shedding, staining her face.

"I went back to get you . . . but you weren't there," I said.

She didn't answer. She didn't even look at me. She had her keys in her hand.

"We need to talk—"

"I don't want to talk." She started to open the door.

I grabbed her by the arm and she tried to pull away. I dug my fingers in deeper. There was no way she could get away from me unless I wanted her to and—I let her go.

"Please . . . you don't need to talk . . . could you please just listen . . . just for a few seconds . . . *please*?"

She was biting down on her lip, fighting back tears. She looked up at me and nodded her head ever so slightly.

"I need to tell you how wrong I was, that there's no excuse for what I did . . . it's just that I love you so much and now . . . now I know that you probably won't ever want to even see me again, or . . ." I burst into tears.

Katie looked shocked. I felt shocked. I tried to stop myself, but I couldn't, the tears came pouring out.

"It's all right," Katie said. She reached out and took my hand. "I'm not going to leave you . . . I'm upset, but I'm not going to—"

The sobbing got stronger, rumbling up from my chest. I couldn't stop it, I couldn't control it.

I heard the door open again and a couple came into the entrance. They were staring at us—staring at me—but I couldn't stop the tears. They turned away, trying hard not to look at me, trying to pretend that they couldn't hear me. They hurried through the entrance and into the lobby.

"I've got to leave. I have to go," I mumbled.

I headed for the door but Katie gripped my hand even tighter. "No, don't go . . . please."

"I have to leave . . . I can't stay here . . . not like this."

"Not here. Let's go up to my apartment. Mom and Joey left right after I did, they won't be back tonight."

Katie fixed us a coffee while I worked hard at fighting back the tears, trying to regain some control. I managed to stifle them back to a sniffle but I still couldn't stop them altogether. Strange, if I'd known that tears would have gotten me up here I would have tried to fake them. But there was nothing fake about this. They were real and painful and came not so much from my eyes as from my gut. I felt awful, and not just for what I'd done to Katie—the thought of not seeing her again, of her not wanting to be with me, of her not loving me was more than I could bear to think about. I could feel the tears starting to overwhelm me again. I couldn't let that happen.

I thought about what my father would have said if he'd seen me bawling like a baby. I didn't need to think very long or very hard to come up with the insults he would have tossed at me—*baby, little girl, no son of mine, acting like your mother.*

I remembered the first time he'd hurled that stuff at me, when Olivia, my dog, died. She was older than God, but I didn't know that. All I knew was that I loved her more than anything and anybody, and she was dead. I could hear my father's clipped, annoyed voice, telling me that he'd hoped for "*a son, not a daughter,*" that I was "*too old to be such a suck,*" that he was "*totally ashamed of me.*" I couldn't have been more than five. Maybe if I had known she was dying, if I could have prepared myself, maybe I could have handled it better, not disappointed him so much or . . . I never cried in front of him again. Even with all that trouble at St. Anthony's Prep. Not a tear.

"Here," Katie said as she handed me a cup of coffee.

I took a big sip. It was hot and sweet and the warmth seemed to melt away the knot that was in my stomach.

"Thanks . . . thanks . . . so much," I said.

"I'm sorry, too."

"You're sorry? You have nothing to be sorry about. It was all me. You didn't do anything wrong. I was just . . . just so . . . so scared," I said.

"Scared of what?"

"Of losing you. That you were going to leave me the way that I've been left—" I stopped myself, but not in time. I'd said more than I should have. I couldn't believe that I'd blurted that out.

"I'm not leaving you. We'll work this out, Evan, but not now." She stood up. "Now, I'm going to shower and change, and then you're going to drop me off at the bakery. I'll only be an hour late if you drive."

I should have been happy. I should have been ecstatic. I hadn't blown it. But something wasn't right. We were still together, but somehow, something was different about her, about me, about us.

I sat there, me looking up and her standing above me, looking down at me, and there was something in her eyes. Instead of a look of adoration, there was pity. And in that instant I realized that I'd made a mistake. I shouldn't have come back, I shouldn't have apologized, I shouldn't have been there. I should have stayed in control. In every relationship there was always somebody who was in charge, somebody with the upper hand, somebody running the show. I'd have to fix that, and fix it soon. My father would have known what to do. But right then and there, I swallowed and looked up at her mascara-stained face.

"Okay," I said. "I'll drive you."

Chapter Thirty-Seven

I picked up the phone and quickly put it back down as if it was dangerous. It *was* dangerous. It was important that I not call her, that she call
me first. During the day it had been easy for us not to talk because she
was doing a double shift and couldn't use her phone. But now . . . she
was off work and either heading home or heading someplace else.

I'd thought about being there outside the employee entrance of
the bakery, waiting, when she got off work. I'd even fantasized about
having some flowers for her. I could just picture how happy that
would have made her—she really was beautiful when she smiled. But
I didn't go, I hadn't done it. I couldn't go there. That would have been
even more dangerous than a phone call.

Driving her home would have been a mistake. Being at the con-
trols of the car wasn't the same as being in control. I would have
been nothing more than her *chauffeur*. I might as well have bought
myself a little cap and stood there to open the back door for her.

I was *nobody's* servant, and there was no way that she could
tell me what to . . . okay, just settle down. She wasn't asking me to be
her servant. She wasn't asking me to pick her up and drive her any-
place. Katie was always just grateful when I did anything for her, but
this was something I wasn't going to do.

If I had picked her up it would have been just like admitting,
again, that I was wrong to have left her at the side of the road in the

rain. Okay, maybe it wasn't something that I was proud of, but it wasn't like I'd been the one to start it. She'd even admitted that she had been flirting. I *never* flirted around her. I'd never cheated on her. And it wasn't like I couldn't have. I could have had any girl in that whole school, any time, but I hadn't. At least, not yet.

I picked up my phone. I didn't have anybody's number, but it wouldn't be hard to find some. I knew last names, and Melody had even mentioned her street name to me. It would have been a simple matter to call directory assistance and get her phone number. I did have Danny's number—I could have just called him and asked him for a couple of numbers. He'd gladly have passed them over. After all, he did owe me. Without that car—without my help—he would have been dead before he even started with Brittney. He *definitely* owed me.

Who knew, maybe Brittney would just hook me up with one of her friends, and I wouldn't even have to make a phone call. It could be all sort of innocent and . . . it didn't matter if it started innocently. No, I couldn't do that, everybody would know soon enough. Between tweeting, Facebook, cameras and cellphones it would be headline news at school by noon the next day. I wanted to *change* the dynamics of my relationship with Katie, not *end* the relationship.

Of course, if that did happen it wouldn't take me long to find somebody new. I'd *win* the breakup, no question. I'd be dating somebody else within a day or two, walking around the school with a little bit of arm candy, while she'd be huddled with her loser friends. She'd be miserable. Lisa would probably be happy, though. Not only would she turn out to be "right" about me, but the way would be clear for her to finally work up the nerve to put a move on Katie. That wouldn't matter to me. I'd move on, quickly, find somebody better and . . . I didn't want anybody else. I just wanted Katie. No, not wanted . . . needed.

I went to put down the phone again and then hesitated. I didn't want to be sitting here, by myself, waiting for her to call. I wasn't some *girl*.

I punched in the number—*Danny's* number. It clicked, rang and then—

"Hey, Evan, what's happening?"

"Hey, Danny. Not much, just wondering what you're up to."

"Trouble, but not serious trouble."

I heard a girl's voice in the background, giggling at his lame little joke. It sounded like Brittney.

"Do you want to do something tonight?" I asked.

"I'm afraid I have my hands a little full . . . well, at least I hope they'll be a little full," he said.

"That's disgusting!" I heard Brittney shout, and then they both started to laugh.

"It does sound like you're busy," I said.

"Maybe we could double. Me and Brittney and you and Katie," he suggested.

"I'm not even going to *call* her tonight," I said. "A man needs some space."

"Gutsy move. Maybe not too bright, but gutsy, I'll give you that much," Danny replied.

"No guts, no glory. Besides, some of us are whipped and some of us are in charge," I said.

"I hear ya," he said. "Although I'd rather be happy than in charge."

I heard slobbery kissing sounds. I was annoyed and a bit jealous all at once, but I shouldn't have been. Let him have his *little* relationship. I knew I could have had Brittney myself, if I'd wanted to. Could have her even now.

"Okay, you have yourself a good night," I said.

"Counting on it. Give me a call tomorrow and maybe we can hang."

"Definitely," I said, but I didn't mean it. "Later."

I hung up. There was no way I was going to call him tomorrow. I'd given him a chance, and if he'd been a real friend he would have . . . did I have a *real* friend? Was *I* a real friend to anybody? Even the people I hung out with from my old school really weren't friends. There were some people I could call to go out someplace with, but there was nobody I could talk to, nobody I could confide in and, more important, nobody I could trust. And tonight there wasn't even anybody here I could pretend was somebody I could talk to. My mother was at some sort of charity gathering and my father . . . well, he could have been anywhere. I was just grateful he was somewhere else.

Katie's mother was gone for the weekend again, but at least she had those two freaks, Lisa and Travis. Even if I didn't call she could still spend the evening with them. She could talk to them. Me, I had nobody. Nobody except Katie.

Again, the urge to call her resurfaced, and this time it was even stronger. I didn't want to be alone. I wanted to be with her—talk to her, spend time with her—but I couldn't. That would have tipped the balance of power even farther in the wrong direction. Tomorrow, I'd give her a call, maybe even offer to take her out for a drive or a coffee. On my terms. But not tonight. Tonight, there would be no contact, no Katie. But then again, just because I wasn't going to be with Katie, that didn't mean she wasn't going to be with me.

I started off for my bedroom but spun around and headed to my father's liquor cabinet. I grabbed a bottle of vodka—one of so many that he wouldn't even notice.

I uncapped it and took a big swig. It burned, but that burning felt good, like it was cleansing me, scouring away my doubts. I took another big hit and settled in at the desk in my room. My computer was already on and I clicked through the files until I found the ones I was looking for—the pictures of Katie.

The first pictures made me smile. She was in those new clothes, looking so beautiful, but so innocent and so happy at the same time. Part of her beauty was that she didn't even know how beautiful she was.

I slowly scrolled through the pictures. With each one there was a little less clothing. But there was also a little less innocence, a little less joy in her expression. How could I have done that to her? How could I have taken that away?

There was an obvious answer. I could delete them. Take them off my computer the way I'd taken them off my phone, and she'd never know that I'd only told her half the truth when I'd said they were gone. It was such a simple solution, it would be done in seconds.

I quickly highlighted all the images except the first picture. Without stopping to think I hit delete and they all vanished. They were gone, except that one image. I was left with the one picture of Katie happy, smiling at me, almost as if she was telling me how pleased she was with what I'd done.

Now all I had to do was go to the Trash and empty it and they'd be gone forever. Gone . . . along with the proof I'd need if she ever accused me of doing anything against her will . . . Wait, I also had the recording. That would be my protection. Not that I'd ever need that from Katie. She'd never do that to me. Or would she?

Forget about the proof. If those pictures disappeared I'd lose even more. They were, in the end, my final power over her. They could be a threat, or at least a way of getting back at her if she ever did dump me. As long as I had the photos, I'd have the ultimate control, the ultimate say. She could end the relationship, but I could decide what happened after that.

I had to think more before I emptied the Trash. I just wished it could be that easy to get rid of all the trash in my life. I took another big slug from the bottle and walked away, leaving my computer behind.

Chapter Thirty-Eight

I slept from the moment I got home from the bakery on Saturday night until late Sunday afternoon. I slept the sleep of the dead. The only reason I roused from my coma was that I had to pee. That, and the apartment buzzer was buzzing itself hoarse. I'd pretty much slept sixteen hours straight, but instead of well rested, I felt drugged and thick-tongued.

"Hello?"

"Katherina, Kate, my darling shrew, is that you, sweetpea? You sound like a large man with a cholesterol problem."

"Travis?"

"Me too!"

"Lisa?"

"Give our girl a pony!" said Travis. "Now, let us up, we have news!"

I glanced around the apartment and groaned. Lisa had been here exactly once and Travis not at all. "Give me a minute to pee and brush my teeth and then I'll buzz you up."

They practically burst through the door when I finally let them in. Travis didn't gasp or anything when he got to my living room so I figured Lisa must have warned him. I mean, the place was pretty much spotless—both Mom and I were obsessively clean. It was just that the furniture must have looked like it cost a

buck fifty, total. I knew that now, after spending so much time at
Evan's.

Anyway, Travis was cool, but Lisa was not. She stood back and
gasped. "Katie! Oh my God! Your knee!"

I could hear my heart ramp up. I'd forgotten that I was still
wearing a nightie.

"I . . . slipped, the night of the party." I caught sight of the
home phone just then. The message light was flashing. Evan. My
iPhone was also vibrating beside my little purse and my shoes,
which were all still on the coffee table where he'd left them when
we came in. It *brrrrr*-ed and lit up again. If it were anyone but Evan,
I could just text him that I'd call as soon as Lisa and Travis left. But
he was psychotic on the topic of my friends. No need to get him
all stirred up again. So, I just watched the phone vibrate.

"Katie?" Travis was frowning.

"Yeah! My knee." I smiled at him. "Too much to drink, I
guess. Doesn't hurt, though. I forgot all about it."

"You didn't drink, remember?" Lisa said, folding her arms.
"I was there as Josh tried to get a drink down you all night, but you
wouldn't budge."

Wow. Was that the way she saw it? Was Josh really being more
than just friendly? Come to think of it, his girlfriend wasn't at the
party. Maybe Evan had caught a whiff of something I was too thick
to see? It just proved that he was right.

"Oh yeah, but it was slippery, remember, it rained. So, what's
the news?"

Travis plopped himself on the couch and thankfully it held,
the couch I mean, you never knew about our furniture. It had col-
lapsed under Joey twice so far. I was barely keeping it together.

"Okay, number one, the most antisocial but hilariously rich

girl in the entire school has agreed to host the cast party on closing night!" Travis clapped and extended his arm to Lisa, who curtsied daintily.

"It's true," she said. "My parents, as you can well imagine, are so stupefied by the idea of me having anyone over that this thing is going to be over the moon, fair warning. They've been talking to *caterers* all weekend!"

"You're kidding, right? I don't believe it! Lisa Chapman is having a party!" I grabbed her by both shoulders. "Who *are* you and what have you done with my friend?"

She groaned and shoved me off. "Hey, what can I say? I loved Friday night, I loved it when the three of us were dancing and we weren't a freak show. We were in without trying. I don't know how it happened, but it was shocking how good it felt. Maybe it's because we're all older and wiser. Things change in grade eleven."

Travis harrumphed.

"And grade twelve. Thing is," she almost looked embarrassed, "I loved it so much that I'm going to throw my own party. Maybe it's a big mistake but I'm prepared to make it!"

"I loved the party too, Lisa." I hugged her. "It was absolutely the very best night of my life."

Until it became the worst.

"Hey!" Travis jumped up and wheedled his way into the hug. "What am I, chopped liver? I'm the one who convinced her to let her parents have it catered. We'll eat like kings after the show, just like they do on Broadway." We threw our arms around him.

"Ummm," he purred. "That feels great, squeeze tighter, girls."

"Travis, that's just the kind of thing that confuses everybody about your sexuality, honey," Lisa mumbled into his shirt.

He gave us each a little extra hug before letting go. "Yeah, well, the line forms to the left on that one, my hot little savant, and I'm leading it."

"Yeah, well, back to the party, the parental units have sort of promised to look the other way for a bit, but along with caterers, there will be servers, and food half our group won't ever have seen before. It'll be weird, but it'll be *my weird* and I'm having it to celebrate . . ." Lisa disengaged enough to elbow Travis.

"Oh yeah, Part *Deux* of the news! So . . . Cooper has been banging the drum loudly, so not only is the woman from the National Academy summer scholarship program going to be there checking you out on opening night on Thursday, but . . . but . . . the assistant dean is in town, and he's coming to the show on closing night, to eyeball *me* for next year's application pool to the Academy and to flag *you* for admission the following year, dear heart!"

"Oh . . . my . . . God!" I squealed. We all squealed. We were pathetic, really.

Lisa grinned from ear to ear. "And I'm just going to get Daddy to buy my way in, because I've decided I want to do something stupendously creative with my life too!"

"Lisa, that is amazing!" I said. "You're throwing a party *and* making positive choices about your future."

"I blame it on the two of you." She shrugged. "Bad influences."

"Let's hug some more!" said Travis.

"Okay, but don't try to cop a feel!"

Just as we embraced again, the door swung open and Mom and Joey walked in. My head exploded as I caught the look on my mother's face. But Joey saved the day.

"Hey! What are we celebrating?" he asked.

"Sorry for just barging in like this, Mrs. Rosario," Lisa said. Then she stepped smoothly in front of me with one angled leg, so that my chewed up knee would not be visible.

"Hey, Mom, Joey, this is Lisa and this weirdo is Travis, my friend and my director."

Joey, God bless his bones, marched over and shook Travis's hand so hard I thought his arm was going to come out of the socket.

"We're coming Friday night, opening night for the paying public! We can't wait to see what you've done. Right, Cheryl?"

Mom smiled and nodded. She wasn't beaming, but she wasn't all pinched-looking either.

"Like your look, kid!" Joey still had a grip on Travis.

"Sir?"

"It's good advertising." Joey nodded. "You're a director, not an accountant, you look arty, you're your own billboard. I like that."

"Speaking of which, we love your new bus shelter photos, Mr. Campana," said Lisa. "My parents are going to be very impressed that I met you." I loved this girl.

Joey puffed up and Mom went to the kitchen. Then, to compound a day of wonders, she called out, "Would you kids like to stay for dinner? Don't worry, Joey made it ahead of time, not me."

I'm not sure I have ever had anyone over for dinner, ever. Not since Nick Kormos, anyway. I'm pretty sure it was never allowed. What was Joey doing to her?

"No thanks, Mrs. Rosario, I've got a lot of prep to do from now on." Travis turned to me. "Get sleep, more sleep. Just afternoon rehearsals this week. I don't want anyone burning out before the first performance." He squeezed my hand and Lisa kissed my cheek. "Love you to bits, Katie."

"Great friends you got there, kid!" Joey called from the dining table when I'd shut the door.

They were.

Lisa, my prompter, discreetly hiding my injured leg, unasked. And Travis, being as happy about someone from the Academy turning up for me as he was for them coming to check him out.

I didn't deserve them.

Wait.

Why not? They *were* great friends, and I promised myself that I *would* deserve them, soon.

"Joey?"

"Yeah, kid?"

"You were super, Joey, thanks."

"Joey?" He grinned. "Call me Mr. Campana."

I felt his smile warming up my back all the way to my room.

Chapter Thirty-Nine

H e was so beautiful in that *I own a sailboat* kind of way, in any kind of way really, and yet, he loved *me*. How great was that?

We didn't have drama on Mondays so Evan and I didn't find each other until lunch. Actually, on that Monday, I'd thought he had a costume fitting scheduled so Lisa and I were chowing down in the Droopy Diaper on Organic Chicken Chili. It felt good. She didn't say anything, but I knew it felt good for her too.

We were reviewing catering themes for her cast party. I finally agreed that Malaysian would be terrific, even though I wasn't at all clear on what Malaysian food was, no matter how many times she explained it to me. I was startled to see Evan lope up the far end of the cafeteria. I was also startled to see that pretty much everyone stopped to sneak a peek, even after all these weeks.

He pulled up a chair across from me and Lisa. I felt her tense up. We hadn't had lunch, just the two of us, since Evan and I had become an item.

"Hey, Lisa, what's up?" Evan lasered her a smile that would have melted a glacier. Instantly, I was afraid. And then, just as instantly, I was ashamed.

"Not much." She shrugged. "Just an FYI, Travis wants me stage left as your prompter Thursday night and Friday night, then, for some bizarre Travis reason, stage right on Saturday night."

"Great!" I said. "I feel calmer already."

"Final curtain calls, closing night bouquets. He's thought of everything."

Evan seemed, if not shocked, at least surprised by that idea.

"Well, let's face it, the prompter's job is all moot, I will never meet two more prepared actors than you guys."

I could tell she was making a superhuman effort to be charming to Evan.

"I do know that tonight, Travis wants you to focus on the capitulation scene, the very last scene. I swear it's the only bit that trips you two up."

Evan threw his arm around me and caressed my shoulder. "Don't know why," he said. "You'd think I'd love to see my woman surrender." He winked at Lisa. "Guess I just have trouble imagining how that would be."

"Yeah." Lisa nodded. "Guess so."

"Total submission, Katie!"

That was Ms. Cooper calling from the back of the auditorium. We were at least an hour into rehearsal and apparently she couldn't contain herself a minute longer and had to jump in on Travis, who in turn jumped up on stage. Hortensio and Lucentio grabbed chairs and sat down.

It was a pretty piece of irony that this bit was the part I had the most difficulty with. Kate the shrew, the volcano, I'd had no trouble accessing right from the start. I *was* her. But with each growing day and every rehearsal, I increasingly tripped over Kate the meek and Kate the well-behaved.

"Katie, you're great, brilliant, etc., etc., but somehow you haven't fully committed to the submission." Travis took my arm and gently moved me away from Evan. "Look, you've bought what he's selling by this point. Petruchio not only wins, but you're glad of it. Commit, Katie. Total, utter submission. You are happily defeated. Got it?"

Defeated?

"He's the prince, thy head, your sovereign, your king. You *owe* him and he *owns* you." Travis leaned in close to my ear, practically kissing me. "Are you an actress or not?"

I nodded and allowed it to happen, the stage, the words, the transformation. My stomach tightened and I was off into Katherina's line 160.

> *I am ashamed that women are so simple*
> *To offer war for rule, supremacy, and sway,*
> *When they are bound to serve, love and obey.*
> *Why are our bodies soft, and weak, and smooth,*
> *Unapt to toil and trouble in the world,*
> *But that our soft conditions and our hearts*
> *Should well agree with our external parts?*

Evan stepped towards me, all proud and glorious. He hesitated and smiled encouragingly, almost secretly so that Travis couldn't see that he was doing it as Evan, not Petruchio. And in that moment, I knew that whatever else was going on, or would happen, I knew that I loved him and always would. He had given me so much. I exhaled.

> *. . . And place your hands below your husband's foot.*
> *In token of which duty, if he please,*
> *My hand is ready to do him ease.*

Evan grabbed me possessively by the crook of my arm. "*Why there's a wench! Come on, and kiss me, Kate.*"

He pulled me into him hungrily. At the exact moment we kissed, Ms. Cooper, Travis, Lisa, Hortensio, Lucentio and the entire backstage crew, including Danny, all stood up and clapped. We'd nailed it. I was his, to do with as he wished. Petruchio and Evan and the entire company knew it, felt it and believed it right then and there.

I *was* an actress, after all.

Chapter Forty

I pulled the car off to the side of the road.

"What are you doing?" Katie asked.

"I thought we'd just stop for a bit. Have a little private time."

"This is hardly private," she said. "It's a public street."

"It's also dark and I don't see any public around. We can have a few minutes to ourselves . . . to talk . . . or whatever."

I could tell by her reaction that she was feeling unsure.

"Dear Katherina, remember your strength is in obedience. Submit to your husband," I said, paraphrasing from our play.

I reached over, put my arm around her and moved forward. She pulled away.

"What's wrong with you?" I snapped, expelling a sudden wave of anger. I could feel her whole body tense. "I mean . . . what's wrong, baby?" This time my voice was soft and soothing and caring.

"It's just that I'm not comfortable. That's all."

"You haven't been very *comfortable* lately at all," I replied.

"I guess it's just all the pressure with the play. I'm scared."

"Scared of what?"

"We're going to be standing in front of hundreds of people, and what if it goes wrong or—"

"It's not going to go wrong. You're going to be brilliant," I said.

"Thanks."

"Maybe this is the point where you should tell me that I'm going to be brilliant as well."

"Of course you are!" she exclaimed. "I just didn't think you needed to hear it. You know how good you're going to be."

I laughed. "That's what I was trying to show you before you pulled away . . . how good I *can* be."

"You know what I mean. You just seem so confident all the time," she said.

"That's the secret. To act confident even when you're not."

"Why would you ever be unconfident? You're so good at *everything*."

"Nobody is good at everything," I said. "Besides, no matter how good you are there are always some people who think you're not good enough."

"Nobody could ever think that of you," she said.

"You should talk to my old man," I snapped, then wished I hadn't. "But I didn't pull over to talk about my screwed up father. How about giving your Petruchio some *comfort* before I drive you home?"

She shook her head. "I just . . . just . . . not here . . . not now."

"There's nothing to worry about. Between the darkness and the tint on the windows nobody could see us, even if there were somebody out there walking, and there isn't."

"Not now. Please. There'll be time later, or, or . . ."

I felt a rising surge of anger, fuelled by a sense of rejection—I pictured opening the door again and pushing her out of the car. "Sure, that's what photos are for," I muttered. Mistake, wrong tense.

Katie's face clouded, confused. "What?"

"Nothing, I didn't say anything." She'd heard but hadn't heard clearly enough.

I pulled out the key and shoved it into the ignition.

"Evan, please, don't be angry with me, *please*."

"What makes you think I'm angry?" I asked through clenched teeth. "Why would my girlfriend pushing me away, rejecting me, not wanting to be with me make me angry?"

"Please, Evan, it's not you, it's me," she said.

"I've heard about people using that line, but I never thought it would be used on me!"

"It's not a line, and it's not you. It's just not the right place," she said.

"Then where is the right place?"

"Some place . . . more private," she said. "Because of the play, my mother isn't going away or else we could—"

"My parents are going out Friday night. Some important charity shindig. You could come over. We'd have the place to ourselves," I said.

She hesitated. "Sure, that would be . . . that would be good."

"Don't sound so thrilled by the idea."

"It's just that I'm going to be so exhausted and—"

"Nobody is asking you to run a marathon. I'm sorry you think it's such hard work to be with me!" I started the car.

"Wait!" she said, putting a hand on my hand. "Maybe we could spend a little time here . . . it is sort of private."

"Don't do me any *favours*."

I put the car in gear and pulled out onto the road. I caught a sideways glance at her expression. She looked surprised, shocked and a little bit hurt. I didn't care. I was back in control. She'd asked to make out and I'd turned *her* down.

We drove along in silence. It was an unspoken contest about not speaking. The first one to speak would lose. I knew that. I was just surprised that either she knew it or she wasn't willing to give in by talking, by apologizing. What exactly was going on here? Hadn't I just reestablished the upper hand?

I pulled up to the curb in front of her apartment.

"Thanks for the drive, Evan."

I'd won.

"No problem. Ever."

She leaned over to kiss me, but I didn't face her. She hesitated and then kissed me on the cheek. "I really love you," she said.

"That's nice." I knew what I was supposed to say, but I wasn't going to say it.

She climbed out of the car and started away. I knew she was close to tears. I hit the button and opened the passenger-side window.

"Katie!" I called out.

She stopped and turned around and came back to the car. She leaned into the window.

"Yes?" she asked, expectantly.

"Do you know why I'm not nervous about the play?" I asked.

"Because you know you're going to do so well?"

I shook my head. "I'm not nervous because I don't care what the audience, or my parents, or Travis or any of them think about my performance. I only care what *one* person thinks . . . you."

I could see her whole expression change—she was still close to tears but they were for a different reason.

"And the sad part is that that person doesn't feel the same way about me," I said. "She cares more about what they think than what I think."

Her eyes filled. I drove away before she could see that she wasn't the only one in tears.

Chapter Forty-One

I pulled into the driveway. Great, my father's car was there—he was home. For a few seconds I thought about just driving away, but there really was no point. He probably wasn't going anywhere tonight.

I turned on the little interior light and looked in the mirror. I used the back of my hand and my sleeve to wipe away the remaining evidence of tears. My eyes were still red, but that could have meant anything. If I was lucky they'd just think I'd been smoking dope.

I opened the front door and my father's voice boomed down the hall. He was angry, giving somebody a piece of his mind. Whoever was on the other end of that phone call was being ripped to shreds and—I heard my mother sobbing. I rushed into the living room. She was on the sofa, and he was standing over her, yelling at her at the top of his lungs.

They both saw me at the same instant. They looked surprised, but he also looked angry, and she looked scared and ashamed.

"What's going on?" I demanded, surprised by my own outburst.

"Just go to your room!" my father yelled. "This is none of your business!"

I started to turn to leave and then stopped. "Mom, are you all right?"

"I told you to go to your room!" he yelled.

He took a few steps towards me. In the past that would have been enough. This wasn't the past. I walked towards him, brushed by, and he grabbed me by the arm and spun me around.

"You really think you're man enough to take me on?" he demanded.

"I don't know. I guess we'll find out."

"Please, don't!" my mother called.

"Shut up!" he yelled at her. "He can't hide behind his mommy forever!"

"No one is hiding. I'm right here in front of you."

"You think I won't hit you?" he screamed.

"Please, I just don't—"

"You think I won't hit either of you!" he yelled, cutting my mother off.

"Do you think I won't hit you back if you do?" I asked. "Do you think I'm going to stand here and let you hit her?" I paused. "I'm not a little kid any more," I said, my voice surprisingly calm.

I put myself directly between him and her.

He laughed. I hadn't expected that reaction.

"Big man. He thinks because he can manhandle a couple of sixteen-year-old girls he can take *me* on. I'll drop you on the spot!"

I felt that sting. Deeply. That was what he wanted, of course. I tried not to let him see it.

"Go ahead," I said, my voice still quiet. "Take the first swing . . . and I'll take the last."

His expression broke—for a brief second his confidence and swagger were gone before he recovered. It was too late, I'd seen it. I balled my fingers into fists and took a half-step closer. He didn't retreat, but he didn't move forward.

"I'm going out," he said. He started for the door.

I felt my whole body relax—I'd *won*—he was leaving and—he stopped and spun around. He looked directly at my mother. "I've said everything I need to say, and if I have to say it again I'll be using more than words."

"You leave her alone or else!"

"Or else what? Or else I'll kick you both out of *my* house? Or else you won't have a car to drive? Or else you won't have money for university?" He sneered. "Don't think that because you stood up to me I'm impressed. You're still just a boy . . . a momma's boy."

He turned and left. My mother started sobbing again. I dropped down to my knees in front of her.

"It's okay," I said softly.

She looked at me. I looked back. I searched for signs that he'd hit her. I didn't see any marks or bruises.

"You don't have to put up with this," I said.

She opened her mouth to say something but instead started to sob even louder.

I wrapped my arms around her. I wanted to tell her that I would protect her, that I'd take care of her, but could I really? And then I thought about what a terrible person he was, and how he treated her this way . . . and then I realized that I wasn't that much different from him. And that was the best reason for hating him . . . and hating myself as well.

Chapter Forty-Two

I blew my nose on a handful of leaves. It was disgusting. I was disgusting. He made me feel disgusting. How did that happen? At least this time, I hadn't done . . . what Evan wanted. But then, I probably should have. He loved me so much and he *needed* me. Evan had never loved anyone like he loved me. He'd said so. In fact, he said it all the time now.

How could I have?

I had hurt him, and I'd hurt him badly. I should have been ashamed for hurting him.

No. I should have been ashamed for letting him hurt me.

I ricocheted ferociously between all different kinds of shame.

So I blew into decaying November leaves to steady myself. That, and I didn't have a Kleenex on me. I couldn't risk getting caught all teared up and snotty by Mom. She'd actually been so much calmer the past few weeks. I couldn't even remember which shift Mom was on this week. What if she was home and wanted an explanation? Why was I crying? I didn't even know, not really. There were so many things mixed into that stew of tears. And there had been so much to cry about lately. Surely that couldn't be right?

I gave one last good blow onto a leathery oak leaf and I wiped my eyes with my jacket sleeve. Then I walked around the block inhaling deeply for good measure. I was almost normal on the second go-round so I finally went up.

The smell of lamb roasting greeted me as soon as I got off the elevator. Well, Joey was there for sure.

"Mom? Joey?" I called as soon as I got in.

"In here, kid." It was Joey.

I hung up my coat and tossed my backpack into my room before making my way to the kitchen. No Mom. Joey had on his standard cooking/realtor uniform, the snowy-white Italian shirt, and what I now know was a silk Hermes tie flung over his shoulder and one of our pathetic tea towels tucked into his belt. This one was a fraying and greying souvenir from Gatorland, Florida. We'd gone with Nick Kormos. Back when we were happy. Before I'd ruined everything.

Noooo. Before *Nick Kormos* had ruined everything.

Joey gave a good-natured wink. "I'm making lamb shanks that are going to blow your mind, kid!" Then he stopped, seeming to take me in for the first time.

"You okay, Katie?"

"Sure!" I gave him my best standing ovation smile, the one I'd been practising in the bathroom mirror ever since I'd got the part. "Absolutely, Mr. Campana. What's a lamb shank?"

"Call me Joey."

"Yes, sir . . . Joey."

He groaned.

"Something's up. I know you got that big opening night in a couple of days and that would send me to the bathroom and keep me there, but I kinda don't think that's it, kid. Is it?"

I sighed and then tried to take it back. You can't take back a sigh.

"Right. You and your fella okay? Not that it's any of my business."

I must have nodded. No one said anything for a bit. No one moved.

"It's just that you get to be a certain age, kid, and . . . well, I'm a guy, you know?"

Huh? I must have nodded again.

I sat down on the kitchen stool. Joey opened the oven door. He basted the lamb. The broth bathed our kitchen in an honest earthy juiciness.

"You gotta understand something, Katie. Not all of us are jerks, you know. Relationships are complicated."

Complicated was right. Something clicked in my head. *That's what photos are for,* he'd said. Evan had removed all the photos from his iPhone, all but that one nice one that we had taken at the beginning. He knew how the pictures freaked me out, reminded me, upset me. So he'd got rid of them! It felt like an ice cube was lodged in my throat. What was the matter with me? This was Evan. Evan *loved* me.

"Like me and your mom. Your mom, well she . . ."

"Gets in her own way?" I volunteered.

Joey nodded and shut the oven door. "She's crazy with fear, and fear makes you do some pretty stupid things, on the one hand."

Mom, afraid? *My* mother? Angry, yes, mean as a snake, and charming when she had to be, but scared?

"On the other hand . . ." He wiped his hands on the towel and examined me for something or other. "On the other hand, sometimes you have to go with your gut, and if it's full of fear, if you're jumpy for any reason, then you gotta cut and run, honey. I meet a lot of people in my business and I gotta be some kind of judge of character. And if you're worried about your guy, Katie, it will not get better."

Our eyes met. He knew. I don't know how he knew, but he knew that something was off with Evan. He hadn't even met him, and somehow, he knew I was afraid.

"Yeah. Sure. Thanks." I nodded, desperate to change the topic. "So, you and Mom?" There was so much buried in those words. I would judge him by the honesty of his answer, not that I had any kind of track record. My "liar alert" appeared to be permanently disabled. Or was it?

Joey folded his arms and sighed. "I'm trying, kid. I can't make any promises, though."

"You wouldn't leave because of me, would you, Joey? Please be honest. A kid can really screw up stuff. I want you to know that I can do better. I can be better."

Joey groaned and reached into the fridge for a Stella Light. "That's your mom talking." I was about to protest, but he put up his hand. "And it's the fear that makes her talk that way. *Her* fear, Katie, not *yours*." He took a deep swig of beer. "Look, I'm crazy about your mom. When she's really herself, there is no one better to be with. I want to take care of her, and you too, if you'll let me, but . . ."

"But she may screw it up."

He nodded. "Speaking of screwing up, hang on for a second, kid, I want to remind myself of something."

Joey pulled out his iPhone, hit a couple of buttons and started talking. "Note to self, don't screw up the Hollanger listing and search. Remember, she hates any memory, no matter how trivial, that reminds her of her humble origins. Stay close to Justin Park and keep the search to nothing less than six bedrooms." He paused. "And only show her that old-money feel. Stay away from the

moderns and anything new, even if it's made to look like it's old."
He hit something and then smiled. "Sorry, kid, I think I just uncov-
ered the secret to a sale, but I like to get it down before I lose it, and
I'm old school enough that I like voice rather than text for that
kind of thing."

Voice.

Evan's voice. In the car, Evan had definitely said, "That's what
pictures *are* for." Not *were* for. Dear God. He'd said that he'd
removed them from his phone. Could they be somewhere else?
There was so much about this stuff I didn't get. What would he use
them for? The single ice cube in my throat multiplied. I shivered.
What could he use them for? I saw myself turning into a "Dateline
NBC" episode. No. Evan *loved* me. I believed it. I believed him. It
was just that he got so angry when things didn't go exactly . . .

"You okay, kid? Look, I know stuff's going on, and it's more
than the play, I . . . it's just that, I've seen, couldn't help but see, uh,
some marks on—"

"So you can record on your phone?" I asked, interrupting
him, stopping him in his tracks.

"Yeah, sure." Joey nodded and frowned at the same time. "You
get this app, the iPhone Recorder. Handy as hell. But Katie, really,
kid, if I can—"

"I've got to go." Joey looked alarmed. "To my friend Lisa's.
She's good with, uh, what I'm going to need." He raised an eyebrow. "I'll be back soon. Cover for me?"

Joey wiped his dry, clean hands on the towel some more.
"I'll say you had to go back to rehearsal and I'll keep a shank
warm, but . . ."

"I promise, I'll let you know if I need you, if I need help."
I practically ran to the hall.

"Hey, kid!" He came after me. "Two things?"

"Yeah, Mist . . . Joey?"

"One, you're a good kid and you deserve a good guy."

"Thanks, uh, Joey. And?"

"And, I *know* you're a *great* actress. Use it."

"Yeah." I nodded and shut the door. "Thanks, Joey."

I had to change buses twice to get to Lisa's. I used the time to rehearse what I was going to say, how I was going to frame it, massage it. Still make him look good. I had an opera in my head by the time she answered the door.

And thank God she answered the door.

Because I was crying good and hard by then. Again. God, I was sick of crying. But, at the same time it was like all that water had finally washed away something. It was like I was coming out of a long, long drowning sleep.

"Katie? What the . . . ?"

"I need help, Lisa." And I stopped crying.

Chapter Forty~Three

"That was pretty amazing," I said to Katie, trying to be heard over-top of the cheering audience as we stood in the left wing, just offstage.

The rest of the cast was already out front taking their bows. There had been a few missteps, but generally things had gone very well—even better than the performance in front of the student audience the day before.

"You're next," Ms. Cooper said to me.

I reached over to take Katie's hand.

"No," Ms. Cooper said. "Just you . . . Katie is last."

"Okay . . . sure . . ." I let go of her hand.

Danny opened the curtain so I could slip through. I took a step out and the audience started cheering, louder than it had for anybody before me. I joined in the gap in the middle of the line of actors and took a bow. The applause got even louder.

I came up from my bow and scanned the audience, looking for my parents. I knew they had some kind of charity gathering to go to but they'd said they still might come tonight. I couldn't see them, but then again, I couldn't see much, and besides, they were only going to come to one performance so maybe it would be tomorrow's. I wondered if my father was going to come at all. Part of me didn't care. But it wasn't a big enough part.

Now the audience was roaring, and they'd jumped to their feet. It took me a split second to realize the reaction was for Katie. I stepped slightly aside and she brushed by me, walked to the very lip of the stage and took a long, low bow as the entire audience seemed to explode. I could feel a wave of sound wash past us. She was the star, and she had been pretty amazing . . . but that much better than me?

Somebody came up to the edge of the stage—he was carrying flowers. It was her mother's boyfriend, Joey. I recognized him from his billboards. His suit, white and silk, was as tacky as his advertisements. He reached up, and she reached down and gave him a hug. Was something going on between them? She released him and stepped back until she was right beside me. She took my hand.

All of us, in one line, took another bow, and the audience, still on its feet, cheered. We took a second bow and the curtain opened up and performers, from each side, started to retreat until only Katie and I were left onstage. I held onto her hand and then pulled her close and gave her a kiss. The audience started cheering and—she pulled away from me.

"Not here," she mouthed.

I released my grip and turned and exited the stage, leaving her alone. I looked back as she took her final bow. I could tell she was drinking in the audience reaction, basking in the warmth of their applause, standing there all by herself. Without me.

Chapter Forty-Four

There was one long, slow moment when the whole world didn't breathe. It was like we were all waiting for that horror-movie climax, for the bloody rain or the scenery to explode. Instead, after forever, people got up on their feet. A standing ovation. The applause came at us in cascading and breaking waves. I waved back and tossed them my sincerest standing ovation smile.

I filled up. Was that what *that* felt like? It was just like I'd imagined, only better.

There was my mother, second row centre. She looked more surprised than anything—that is, until Joey turned to her before making his way to the edge of the stage. When Joey glanced at her, my mother instantly transformed into a woman who trembled with pride, overcome with emotion. Now *that* was a performance.

No wonder I was good. I *got* that. I *got* my mom. She stood and cheered like she was going to burst a kidney. And despite everything, despite knowing better, I hoped. She clapped and I was hopeful. What the hell, false hope was better than no hope at all, right? And I needed all the hope I could get.

I shivered and then smiled some more.

The audience went wild when Evan kissed me. Both times. First as Petruchio, growling, *Why, there's a wench! Come on, and kiss me, Kate*, and they went even wilder when he tried to kiss me at our curtain call. So this was what a "golden couple" looked like.

He pulled me to him. More applause. Evan was proud of me. That, at least, was honest and true, and knowing it almost broke me. I pulled away. I could not veer off the plan. Not let Evan get me. Not let my love for him get me.

We were headed back to his place within the hour. I couldn't take my eyes off of him in the car. Evan was so pumped and stoked and . . . beautiful.

"Man, you were good! I knew you would be. But still, Katie, wow, you were unbelievably good! You can never doubt it again."

One arm lay on the armrest. The other was casually draped over the steering wheel, caressing it. In profile, Evan Campbell was arresting. Especially when he smiled and his dimples flared. The cut of his jaw, the warm, sweet crook of his neck. His dark-blond hair curled at the nape, unruly. He hated that. I loved it.

Evan turned to me, shaking his head. "Just so brilliant, baby."

My heart tried to break free.

He bowed elaborately as he opened my car door when we got to his house. "My kingdom is your kingdom."

I was struck yet again by the sheer whiteness of his home, by the purity and calm it seemed to represent. Even now that I knew better. I was beginning to clue in that his father was demented and that his mother was just plain weak. But it was still new to me, this whole concept of how could something look one way and yet, totally, be another. You looked at Mom and me, at where we lived, and you expected trailer trash drama, but Evan? In *that* house, with *those* parents?

"Are you sure they're out for the night?"

"Yeah, I promise, they weren't at the performance so they won't be here now. You notice, no car." He shrugged. "They're still probably at a reception with one of my dad's clients."

Evan tossed my coat, my Value Village special, onto what I'd been told was an Eames bench in the foyer. It made my coat look like crap.

"They'll be at closing tomorrow for sure. Maybe," Evan said.

How could you not be at your son's opening night? Evan's hair fell into his eyes when he tried to smile it off. I saw a whole play in that smile. There was the little boy, the nine-year-old waiting for his parents to pick him up at boarding school, always the last ones to arrive. There he was trying to put on a brave and charming face in front of an increasingly annoyed staff member who was eager to leave, but had to wait because of "the Campbell boy."

"Want something to drink?"

I shook my head. Even now, after all the times I had been there, I was too nervous to eat or drink anything in all that white.

Evan sauntered into the kitchen. I heard him open up the fridge and he came back in carrying a Heineken. He took a swig and threw his arm around me with such careless grace that it made me forget to breathe.

"Want to go to the family room? You like that better than the living room."

Where would his laptop be?

"No!" I stopped, and he raised an eyebrow quizzically. "I've never seen your bedroom."

"Hmmmm . . ." He growled and then nuzzled my ear. "That's my girl."

The stairs were a major work of art all on their own. They'd freaked me out from the first time I saw them. The actual steps were made of glass, fastened together with polished steel rods. There were no risers, only air separated one step from another. Every footfall was unnerving. I grabbed on to the chrome handrail like I was personally holding up the house. At some point, Evan turned around, frowned and loped back down. "It's okay, I've got your back." And with that he stood beside me placing his hand gently, but so protectively, at the small of my back. I swear I would have followed him anywhere.

No one had ever made me feel the way Evan made me feel. No one had made me believe in myself the way he did.

We walked into his room together. In this house of white, Evan's room was saturated with rich colour. Sage greens, harvest gold and all that dark wood. It was very male, yet not oppressively so. There was an entire ebony bookcase filled with ribbons and trophies.

"Evan, so many trophies, so many awards! My God! Why didn't you tell me? You're like this superstar! Rugby, debating, soccer . . . is there anything you don't excel at?"

Evan shrugged, clearly surprised by my reaction. "My mother's decorator did that. It's more for her than me. None of that stuff's important."

I fell in love with him all over again.

"This is." Evan walked over to his desk, which was at the far end of the room in front of a massive floor-to-ceiling window. He picked up a silver-framed copy of the playbill Lisa had designed for our production of *The Taming of the Shrew*. The photo had been taken during dress rehearsals. Because Lisa had taken it, I was prominently featured, with Evan and the rest of the cast more in the background. "Now *this* is important!" he announced.

I threw myself into him and he caught me, he was that strong. It felt like I had the world in my arms. I loved touching him and inhaling the singular ocean smell of him. Evan pulled me into him even tighter. If we just didn't let go . . . if we just stayed like that, maybe all that was bad and broken around us, and in us, wouldn't matter. We'd make it.

And then I saw the laptop, his MacBook Air. I let go. "You know," I reached up and kissed his dimple, "I would love, love, love a coffee from that fancy machine you guys have in your kitchen."

"Anything for my star. What would you like—a cappuccino, a latte?"

"You can do that, really? I'd be so happy with cappuccino, thanks so much!"

Evan shook his head.

"What?" I asked.

"No one makes me feel like you do. It's like all I have to do is cross the street and you think I'm amazing," he said.

I turned casually, to put the photograph back, so he couldn't see me tensing up. "Because you *are* amazing," I said under my breath.

"One skinny cappuccino coming up. I know that's how you like it." Evan bounced off.

As soon as I heard him on the stairs, I went to my purse and turned my iPhone recorder on. Then I put the phone back in my purse and placed it beside the computer.

"I'm opening up the laptop the way you taught me, Lisa." He was far enough away that I was sure he couldn't hear that distinctive Mac chime when it turned on. I scrolled to the bottom and found the Finder. We only had PCs at school, so Lisa had had to give me a super-intensive tutorial on it.

"Okay," I whispered in the direction of my purse, "I'm scrolling, scrolling, scrolling. Hang on. I'm typing my name into the search field. Nothing! I was right, Lisa!"

But Lisa had said that was no guarantee, so I moved to iPhoto and kept scrolling. Then I found a huge stash of picture files. My heart pounded in my throat. I must have whipped through two million photos of kids in uniforms, rugby games, New York and what looked like places in Europe. Girls, lots of beautiful girls in fabulous tight dresses at what appeared to be fabulous clubs. I felt dirty and jealous at the same time.

But there was nothing, nada, zip, zilch, zero! No Katie photos! Evan *had* gotten rid of them! Just like he'd promised. I unfurled like a blossom opening to the sun. I loved him so much I thought my heart was going to implode.

Trash.

"Okay, okay," I whispered to my purse. "I know you told me I have to check the Trash. It's not really gone until it's deleted from the Trash. Got it." I dragged the little arrow down to the right and scrolled down to the trashcan icon. There were pictures. Only one file. *Katie.* I clicked.

And there I was.

The room swivelled. Posing. Dear God. I couldn't have . . . how . . . I didn't have . . . I didn't remember that part. I didn't, couldn't, when? I was going to be sick. I put my hand over my mouth, gagged, and kept scrolling. They were sick. I stopped, hypnotized by the grotesqueness of one. The one where I . . .

"What are you doing?" Evan was at the door.

I was in such a rage that coherent words were impossible to pluck out and form. "Lisa said . . . she said, said you'd still have . . ."

He saw the screen and then he saw what was on it. There I was, in all my glory, on our cheap, threadbare carpet in front of our even cheaper plywood coffee table, surrounded by the tumblers from Wal-Mart and the throw cushions from Costco. And even with all that stellar competition, I managed to look like the cheapest thing there.

"Lisa is a jealous lesbo . . ."

"No! Stop! That's a lie, and you lied. You still have the pictures. She said you would. They're so ugly, Evan. They're disgusting! You're disgusting for keeping them!"

"No, see baby . . ." He put the coffee cup down and walked towards me. I moved back even farther into the desk, grabbing my purse. "I've been burned in the past. It's why I'm at the school."

I did not move. I did not blink.

"Tamara Nivens, at St. Anthony's, stupid little . . ." Then he stopped himself. "We all got high. Her too. And sure, I was seeing someone else, but Tamara was all over me, couldn't get enough." He stopped and looked at me like I could see the movie that was playing in his head. "Yeah, sure, there was a bunch of us there and things got out of hand, 'cause we were stoned. She was after me all term."

My mind ricocheted back to Nick Kormos. *You tell your mom and I'll just say that you were asking for it. Begging for it.* My heart stopped beating.

"So sure, I did it, and maybe we had an audience, but she couldn't prove it was me specifically. The only reason I got drummed out of the school was because her old man had bigger ones than my old man."

His hand, Evan's beautiful hand, clenched and unclenched.

"But you *did* do it?" I asked.

"Sure I did. You're not listening. She *wanted* it. It was a performance and we were the stars. She just got jumpy about her reputation and took it out on me."

His face clouded and I gripped my purse. I stepped towards the door and the boy I loved stepped towards me.

"You kept the photos, Evan," I whispered.

"I had to!" he yelled. "I had to. What if you decided to run to someone, Cooper, someone at school? It would have been twice. That could be bad for me, see? I needed a guarantee."

"No. No more!" Not one more guy was ever going to touch me wrong, or hurt me or mess with my head. Not Evan, not Nick Kormos, not anyone else again. "You don't need a guarantee. You need help, Evan! You're sick!"

"Shut up and stop whining, I said I had to!" His eyes flared, he was unrecognizable. "You're all alike, manipulative tramps!" He glanced back to the computer screen. "There's the proof, you're a tramp!"

But this boy *had* hurt me, had taken photos I couldn't begin to remember, and made me do things that I was not ready to do. This boy had thrown me out of a car like just so much garbage. And I *loved* this boy?

"And *you*, Evan, are a pig."

He slapped me so hard I fell over.

We both heard the front door of the house open.

"Hi, Evan. Sweetie, we're home. How did it go?"

I heard his father muttering darkly, "Evan?"

Evan turned to me, eyes wild with, what . . . fear, horror?

"Oh God, Katie, I'm so . . . oh God!" He dropped to his knees. "Katie . . ."

I reached over to the computer and hit the delete button and emptied the Trash. The pictures vanished. I got up and ran past him, dazed and dumb, but coherent enough to get down those stupid steps and past his very stunned parents. I had my purse and my iPhone but there was no use pretending, even now. God help me.

My coat was still in the house.

My heart was still in the house.

Chapter Forty~Five

The whole evening felt like a blur, or like I was in a fog. I stood, stunned, and listened as Katie gave her soliloquy. She had been perfect, and I'd been missing lines all night, or not delivering them with the power or the emphasis that they needed. It was bad enough missing lines without having Lisa, standing in the wings, being the one to feed them to me. I almost would have preferred being lost and screwing up to being indebted to her. I could tell that she was enjoying watching me squirm, knowing that I was dependent on her. And I could tell that she knew what had happened between Katie and me. She knew. And I was positive she wasn't the only one.

It was one of the hardest things I'd ever done in my life to show up that night. I'd called her all day long, non-stop, on both phones. She never picked up. Why? How could she ignore me? How *dare* she! I'd waited until the last possible moment. But what other choice did I have? My parents were going to be in the audience, everybody was going to be there. Besides, if I didn't show up, would I ever have another chance with Katie? Smacking her was one thing, but screwing up her big chance . . . that she'd never forgive me for.

I tried to portray Petruchio with power, as someone confident, in charge, a man with a plan to diminish, dominate and control. There was still power in the scenes, but it wasn't coming from me, and it wasn't power *over* her. Something had shifted. I could feel it, and

I knew Katie could feel it too. Was it obvious to anybody else? Even if it was, they wouldn't know why. They'd think that it was just a reflection of the acting, and not the offstage drama.

I was supposed to be taming this girl, but I was almost afraid to let our eyes meet. When I looked at her face I could see a slight swelling, the bruising hidden beneath all the stage makeup. Did anybody else see it, or was it just me, because I knew where to look, why to look?

If I could have taken back one thing, just one thing in my entire life, it would have been that. I'd never meant to do it, hadn't thought, or questioned. I'd just reached out and struck her. I'd felt so much anger, so much hurt. Thank goodness I hadn't hit her harder. It wasn't much more than a glancing blow. Really.

"*And place your hands below your husband's foot; In token of which duty, if he please, My hand is ready; may it do him ease,*" Kate said.

She stopped talking. There was silence. Had she forgotten her line or—

"Why there's a wench!" Lisa hissed.

No, it was my line next!

"*Why there's a wench! Come on, and kiss me, Kate!*" I said.

We both knew what was to happen next. For a split second I hesitated—she hesitated too. Then we came together and kissed. It felt so right, so natural. I could feel more than her lips against mine, I could feel her *soul*. I held her longer than we ever had before, and she didn't pull away. I could hear the reaction of the crowd.

I released her and we separated ever so slightly. I looked into her eyes for the first time that night, deep into her eyes, and I could still see love, still see hope.

Now, what I needed more than anything in the whole world was to just have her sit down and talk to me—no, I just needed her to sit down and *listen* to me. I knew if I could get her alone in a room I could convince her, say the words she needed to hear to forgive me this one more time. She'd done it before, so why wouldn't she do it again? I'd just have to be that much nicer, that much better to her this time. I'd already sent flowers—her favourite flowers—they'd be waiting for her in her dressing room backstage, along with a note. And then I'd buy her something special, something expensive, and I'd be sure to tell her how much I loved her, how much I needed her. It wasn't even that I was lying, or trying to manipulate her. I *did* love her. I *did* need her. And I was sure that she still did love and need me. I was just terrified that I loved her *more* and needed her *more*.

The final line was delivered and the crowd went wild and the curtain fell. I felt a sense of relief. I turned to speak to Katie but she wasn't beside me. She was off to the far side, standing beside Lisa and Travis, her back to me.

The applause practically pushed the curtain back as each successive line of characters came forward and out front for their curtain call. I kept looking at her, but nobody even glanced in my direction. It wasn't like she was ignoring me, it was like she didn't even know I existed. But I knew better. I'd felt her lips, looked deep into her eyes. I still had a chance. But instead of relief or joy, I felt that sense of anger rising in my chest. I tried to stamp it back down. I couldn't afford anger. I needed to at least be in control of *me*. There was no way you could ever control anybody else if you weren't in control of yourself.

"Evan, your turn."

I looked up—it was Travis.

"It's your turn, the crowd is waiting . . . Katie is waiting."

She stood at centre stage, waiting for me and then the stage crew to open the curtain so we could walk out front. She held her hand out and she gave me a smile, that incredible smile, and I knew in that instant that she'd forgiven me, and my heart soared! Not that I deserved it, but she'd found it in her heart to forgive me!

I bounded across the stage, practically flying, my feet hardly hitting the boards and I took her hand and, "Katie, we have to talk—"

"Not now," she said, cutting me off. "After, there'll be time."

We walked out and the applause was deafening, louder, more powerful than anything I thought I'd ever felt. The whole auditorium was up on its feet. And while I knew that it was more for her than for me, I also knew that she was *mine*, so really, it was for me.

We joined the line and took our first bow. The house lights had come partway on and I looked out, searching for my parents. I'd glanced at them a couple of times during the performance but hadn't really seen them in the dark, I just knew where they were. Now I could see them clearly. They were only a few rows back, and they were both on their feet, clapping!

We took our second bow, and then I looked directly at my father and our eyes met. He gave me a little smile and then raised one hand to his chest, turned it sideways and gave it a little wobble. "That was just okay," he said with that one little gesture.

My knees buckled slightly and my head started to spin. I think if I hadn't been held up by hands on both sides I might have tumbled over.

My eyes were still on him, unable to look away, when he turned and walked up the aisle. My mother, a look of shock on her face, then scrambled after him as the rest of the crowd continued to cheer.

I suddenly realized that it was now just Katie and I on the stage, and I had to walk away, leaving her alone to drink up the applause. I went to let go of her hand.

"No," she said. "Stay. I wouldn't be here without you."

Unbelievable. After everything I'd done she wanted me to be with her.

I held onto her and we took one more bow, together, and then we turned, as one, and left the stage behind.

We were instantly surrounded by a crush of people, talking, laughing, celebrating. People took turns hugging her, and some even hugged me. They didn't know what I'd done, or if they did they understood. Somehow they understood. It wasn't really all my fault, and I hadn't hit her that hard, and I hadn't meant it, and I was sorry and I was going to beg for forgiveness, and she *did* forgive me—I already knew that. That meant I could say what I was going to say, but I could still salvage a little pride, a little piece of control, because, despite what I'd done, and how much I needed her, I knew that she still needed me.

"Evan, come with me," she said, and she led me away through the crowd.

Chapter Forty-Six

❤

On Saturday, December 5, at the close of the closing night, the first person I saw spring to his feet was Mr. Campbell. He was, in a way, a bizarre mirror image of my mother from the night before. That rattled me, and I popped out of myself. People were standing and applauding. Mr. Campbell was standing and applauding. I just stood and wondered, did he smack around his pretty wife? And if so, how much? Evan had never come right out and said so.

I touched my cheek. I wasn't even aware of doing it until I made contact. It still hurt. Then I saw Mr. Campbell give Evan the universal hand sign for "pretty mediocre." Evan gripped my hand tighter as we bowed. I snuck a glance at him. He smiled at the audience, acknowledging our standing ovation, but he looked ruined.

And that made me sick.

Evan and I made our way through the gauntlet of hugs and hollers and congratulations backstage and then along the hallway to my dressing room, which was really our guidance counsellor's office.

Ms. Cooper caught us along the way. She was levitating. She introduced me to this guy, Mr. Oudette, from the National Academy. I think he said nice things and that an Academy teacher had been at the opening performance and had also raved. Mr. Oudette said that they would be in touch, or that they'd send stuff in the mail, or they had left it with Ms. Cooper, I don't know . . . something. I hoped that Ms. Cooper was paying attention. It was like I was underwater, like my life was somewhere over there, I could see it, just out of reach. There I was, telling Travis to give me a few minutes to change and clean up before we headed over to Lisa's for her big bash. I knew that was me talking, but I was disconnected from myself. Thank God I was there for the play. The underwater thing didn't happen until it was over.

The end.

Fear?

No.

Unendurable sadness.

Mr. Suta's office was a two by four at the best of times. Now, we barely had room enough to turn around. Travis had rigged up a screen for me to change behind and brought in a coat racks for the costumes. I'd lugged in all of my makeup and hair stuff, which crowded against Lisa's mother's massive magnifying mirror and Mr. Suta's inbox and pencil-sharpener.

Evan shut the door. It was as if we'd stepped into a vacuum. The sound of nothing greeted us.

Shhhh . . . listen, Katie, that is the sound of your heart breaking.

Evan had not said a word from there to here. I don't think he trusted his voice. Shame, fear and hope had chased each other across his handsome face all through the play. He was supposed to be the conquering Petruchio, but instead a seventeen-year-old boy wanting forgiveness had turned up.

He disappeared behind the screen and reappeared with an armload of orchids swathed in cellophane and wrapped in an elaborate pink satin ribbon. Wrong on all counts.

"These," he gulped, "are my desperate plea for forgiveness. I am so, so sorry. Sorry and ashamed. It will never happen again, Katie. This I can promise you. I love you too much to ever risk losing you, if you can only forgive me this one last time."

He held out the flowers. His right arm was shaking.

"I don't like orchids, Evan."

His face crumpled and then reddened. "Yes you do, they're your favourite!"

"No. *You* decided that they were my favourite flower. I've decided that I love lilacs best."

"Lilacs! That's nuts, they're out of season, and you can't even buy them when they're in season." He tossed the bouquet into the corner. I now knew that an arrangement like those orchids would have cost close to a couple of hundred dollars. I did not react. Instead I stepped behind the screen and started to change.

"Okay." Evan raised his voice as if the screen made it harder for me to hear. "If it's lilacs, it's lilacs. Now we both know, right? You didn't even have a special flower when I first asked. Remember?"

True, back in September, like all the years before, it had taken all of my energy just to stay invisible. Favourite flowers? Clothes? Acting? That was for girls who deserved to take up space in the world.

I smiled as I pulled on the blue cashmere sweater that Lisa had "loaned" me so long ago. "You're right." I slipped into my jeans. "You taught me a lot, Evan. About myself, about . . . so much." I was talking too loudly too. Funny what being blind to the other person does to your delivery. As soon as I zipped up I headed straight for the makeup mirror.

"Look, I'll buy you a truckload of lilacs, even if I have to fly them in myself. Just forgive me." Then he stopped and smiled.

The core of me warmed, he was that gorgeous. "What is it?"

"You wore that outfit on our first date."

Evan waiting by the movie poster. Evan coming early so I wouldn't worry or have to wait. The movie, the Mexican restaurant and me spending the whole night fretting about how I was going to pay for my half. That was a different girl. He *had* taught me so much. The whole school *saw* me now. I *deserved* to take up space in the world.

I gingerly applied the cold cream and tried to wipe off the makeup as gently as I could.

Evan inhaled so sharply, I thought he had cut himself.

The swelling had largely subsided by this morning, but the bruise was already transforming into a kaleidoscope of reds, blues and purples. "Don't worry," I said. "I'll reapply street makeup. But Travis and Lisa have seen it."

"God." He shook his head. "I don't know where to go or what to do with the . . . you were right, I *am* a pig." He fell more than sat in the chair.

"Petruchio never apologizes," I pointed out.

"But Evan Campbell does. And Petruchio does confess to Baptista that he loves Kate. Remember? *I love her ten times more than e'er I did.* That's true for me, Katie. I'll prove it. I'll spend the rest of my life proving it to you. Just forgive me, this one last time."

"Words and flowers." I stared at my face. Even the little swelling that was left made me look lopsided and freakish. "Did you think you *were* Petruchio, Evan? That you could manipulate, bully and smack *me* into submission? Tame me, like when Bianca asks about the "taming-school" and Tranio admits that Petruchio is the master of it? Did that sound irresistible to you, Evan? Was it too tempting for someone like you to turn someone like me into the worshipping, mindless plaything?"

"Me?" He snorted. "Get over yourself, Katie. The play's gone to *your* head, not mine."

Evan stood up, and I was aware of how much of the room he occupied. I wouldn't be able to get past him, to the door. When he got big like that, he took up all the oxygen.

"You were no Katherina when I met you. Don't *you* confuse the roles and real life. Katherina is power and guts and—"

"All that I am *now.*" I put down the cleaning sponges and lifted my face to him and made him look. He sat back down. "Thanks in part to you, Evan."

His face actually lit up under the makeup.

"What I mean is, you need help. Your father . . . Get help, Evan."

"Sure!" He nodded. "I get that. Absolutely. In fact, in my pocket," he patted his grey tights. "My pants pocket, I mean. I brought the card of a therapist. Dr. Grimmel, I think." Evan nodded to himself. "They gave it to me at St. Anthony's and I never called, but I'm going to call him now." He nodded some more, trying to convince me, or himself? "Yeah, I brought the card to prove it to you. I'll go see him for you."

"See him for you, Evan, not for me."

"Yeah! For sure! I meant that, of course!" He crossed and uncrossed his legs, his arms. He seemed uncomfortable in his costume and in his body.

"I'd do anything for you, Katie. It didn't start out that way, I admit it, but that's how it is now. You give me courage. You give me . . ." he whispered, "you give me everything. I have never loved anyone like I love you." He put his head in his hands. "I have never been loved by anyone like I have been by you."

He had me there. I stood up but didn't say anything. Then Evan Campbell started to cry. His lovely, powerful shoulders contracted and heaved. Tears ran freely down his face. "Please,

Katie . . ." His eyes were the colour of an angry ocean. "Please . . ."

And I couldn't catch a breath. He'd cried before. He reached for me and I stepped back. It, he, reminded me of something. I searched for the memory, still dizzy with confusion. All that sobbing, all that pain. You'd do anything, absolutely anything to stop it, to make it better.

Found it. My mother cried like that, just exactly like that.

"I do forgive you, Evan, but we're done. I don't want to be with you any more. You will never hurt me again."

"No!" Again, he snapped. It stopped me in my tracks. "Liar, I don't believe you!"

There was a knock on the door.

Travis stuck his head in and I bent down to the mirror, playing with foundation, trying to cover up my cheek, even though he already knew the bruise was there.

"Hey, no rush, you're our star and all. Just checking on when you guys will be—"

"Evan can't come to the party," I said.

Evan's head shot up. Thankfully, Travis could see only the back of it. His tears dried up even as his face darkened. I knew that look. He was furious.

"His folks are planning something special." The lie rolled out easily. "Come back for me in five, though, okay?"

"You got it!" Travis looked at Evan, and looked back at me. I nodded and he shut the door. I had a feeling that he was going to wait right on the other side of the door even if we took all night.

"Who is he?" demanded Evan.

"Who is who? *Travis?*"

"The other guy! There's another guy, isn't there? From the party? Josh! I'll kill him."

I shook my head. "There's no one, Evan. We're just over. Finished."

"You're lying!" The rage was building within him. I knew now how it came at him in little waves, building and building until he had to act or drown.

"Nobody just leaves me."

Evan opened and closed his fists, got up and circled the chair. He looked to the ceiling as if some kind of answer was written up there.

"Of course, you deserve the best kind of guy." The words came out measured, controlled. "You deserve the best, and I promise that I will rise to the occasion. I can be the boy, no, the *man* you deserve, Katie. All I need is *one* more chance. I love you more than I thought I could love anyone. I can't be without you. I'll do anything, *please*, baby."

I felt like I was a shaken snow globe, except that someone had replaced all the tiny snowflakes with tiny shards of glass. How could he be that gentle and vulnerable and still be a Petruchio, still be a monster?

I stood up and faced him. "I don't want you to call, touch or contact me in any way." Evan reacted as if he'd been jolted. "If you bother me in any way, shape or form, even if you think you are charmingly trying to win me back, I will find that poor girl you confessed to molesting, and I will give her the tape."

He stepped back, puzzled.

"This tape, Evan." I reached for the iPhone and pressed.

"*Yeah, sure, there was a bunch of us there and things got out of hand, 'cause we were stoned. She was after me all term. So sure, I did it, and maybe we had an audience, but she couldn't prove it was me specifically. The only reason I got drummed out of the school was because her old man had bigger ones than my old man.*"

"Stop it!" he spat.

And I jumped despite myself. Then I pressed cancel. "Both Lisa and Travis have a copy. Between that, her record of complaint and your expulsion file, you could find yourself in deep enough that even your father's best connections won't be able to clean it up for you." Evan was shaking. "Never mind the prospect of having to tell your father that it's all back again." He had gone white under all that stage makeup. "Stay away from me. Do you understand?"

"Why would you do this? Why are you doing this? Why do you want to destroy me? I love you, Katie. There is no one else for me but you. I'd do anything for you, anything. Why?" His eyes filled, but didn't spill over.

"Do you understand?" I asked.

"I understand, but I don't believe that you don't love me. Not for a minute."

"I don't."

"Let me hold you," he pleaded.

"No."

"Let me hold you one last time. Dear God, Katie. That's all I ask. I promise, I'll never go near you again, or contact you in any way. You leave me no choice. You're blackmailing me." He smiled. "Didn't think you had it in you." Evan held out his arms.

I had no will, no choice but to go to him, to fall into his chest and be held. Us against the universe. My boyfriend still smelled like a beach. I disintegrated.

"I love you, so much." He placed his hand at the back of my head, tenderly. Then he kissed the corners of my eyes. "Tell me you don't love me and make me believe it, and I will never go near you again." Evan wrapped his arms around me and almost made the world go away.

I would never be held like that again. My first love.

He kissed my hair. I breathed him in once more and then pulled back and shook my head. "We're done, Evan. You ruined it. Get help for you, not me, because I do not love you any more. It's gone, you beat it out of me. It's not there. No one will ever lay a hand on me again."

He flinched. I looked up at him, clear-eyed and fierce.

"No, Evan, I do *not* love you."

He let go.

I grabbed my purse and my coat. I picked up the flowers and put them in his arms and then placed the iPhone on top of the flowers.

"Do you get it? Do you believe me?"

He nodded. "Yeah." I could barely hear him.

"Good," I said. "Because I'm late and my public awaits!"

With that I opened the door, stepped out and put my arm around a startled Travis. He squeezed my hand tight and mouthed, "Bravo!" Together we pranced down the empty school hall as if we were Dorothy and the Scarecrow winding ourselves around the Yellow Brick Road.

I was incredibly proud of myself.

Now *that* was a performance!

I didn't even start crying until we got to the car, and then, of course, I couldn't stop.

Dear Reader,

The Taming deals with issues that are dark and difficult. While we found the book challenging, we both truly enjoyed the writing and the interaction involved in two writers working in union. Really though, this book was the product of more than just the two of us. We would like to extend our thanks to Deb Ellis, Phillipa Sheppard, Marie Campbell, Catherine Marjoribanks, Amy Black, and, of course, that Shakespeare guy.

While we're glad when teachers and other adults like our books, we're even happier when children and young adults like them. Those are the people we write for. We want to know what you thought of our book—what did you like, what didn't you like, what would have made the book better, and what do you think we should write about next?

Email Eric at ericwalters@uniserve.com and Teresa at teresatoten@gmail.com.

We promise that we will read your email. Your opinion doesn't just matter to us—it matters a lot.

All our best,
Eric and Teresa